The Search for Jacob's Pillow

The Search for Jacob's Pillow

A Scottish Historical Novel

H. David Brown

authorHOUSE®

AuthorHouse™
1663 Liberty Drive
Bloomington, IN 47403
www.authorhouse.com
Phone: 1-800-839-8640

First published by AuthorHouse   07/05/2011

ISBN: 978-1-4634-2307-0 (sc)
ISBN: 978-1-4634-2306-3 (dj)
ISBN: 978-1-4634-2305-6 (ebk)

Library of Congress Control Number: 2011911553

Printed in the United States of America

MAP OF SCOTTISH LOCATIONS

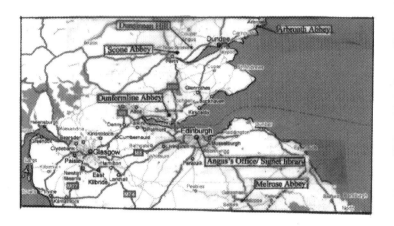

AREA OF 14TH CENTURY CRUSADES

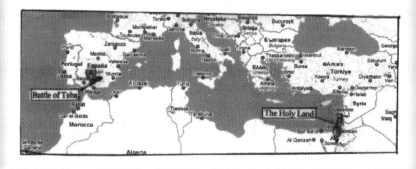

Prologue

Kenneth MacAlpin was crowned the first king of Scots in AD 847. During the coronation, MacAlpin sat upon the legendary Stone of Destiny, that stone being positioned atop a small mound called Boot Hill located near ancient Scone Abbey. The remains of this abbey can still be viewed within its own grounds close by the River Tay, located a few miles upstream from the modern city of Perth in central Scotland.

All ancient kings of Scots, thirty-one in number, were crowned in like manner to MacAlpin until the year 1296. In the summer of that year, an English king named Edward I, more commonly known as Longshanks, led a large English army north to invade Scotland. This invincible army overwhelmed the Scots. After plundering the devastated nation, Edward returned south to London, taking with him the ancient and highly symbolic Stone of Destiny, and had it installed underneath the English coronation seat located in Westminster Abbey. The stone remained there for over seven hundred years.

Recently Scotland regained its own devolved parliament, which essentially deals with Scottish affairs within the United Kingdom. Before the opening of that parliament, and as a gesture of goodwill accompanied by considerable pomp and ceremony, the Stone of Destiny was returned to Scotland. The stone now lies in Edinburgh Castle alongside the ancient Scottish crown jewels. But the question remains, as it has for many centuries, is this "lower old red sandstone" artifact weighing some four hundred pounds really the same ancient stone used during the Scottish kings' coronations before the late thirteenth century?

Tradition and ancient descriptions affirm the stone used during coronations at Scone came from Jerusalem around the fourth century and was hewn from marble found inside the Dome of the Rock before the arrival of Saladin. These early descriptions indicate a stone quite dissimilar in shape and color to the stone currently on display in Edinburgh Castle. The stone originating in the Holy Land was described as being made of white marble and carved with decorative figures. Jewish tradition also affirms the old description and indicates the stone was originally part of a pedestal of the Ark of the Covenant. The questions, "When was a switch of stones made, and where is the original stone now?" remain unanswered.

With three months to anticipate the arrival of King Edward's army at Scone, the monks had ample time and incentive to make a switch to protect the ancient stone. Such a substitution could have been instigated by the abbot of Scone, who served as the stone's custodian. However, there are other theories.

On Christmas Day 1950, four Scottish students, inspired by nationalistic sentiment, stole the stone from under the Coronation Throne in Westminster Abbey, dumped it in the trunk of a car, and drove off with it. Four months later on April 11, 1951, the stone was found lying on the altar of Arbroath Abbey located only forty miles due east of Scone. The Abbey clergy informed the police, and shortly after the stone was returned to Westminster Abbey and again placed under the Coronation Throne. There it remained until its return to Scotland on November 30, 1996. This date, St. Andrew's day, is of special significance to Scots the world over, as St. Andrew is Scotland's patron saint. St. Andrew is also the patron saint of Greece and Russia.

The students could have carried out a switch of stones while the heisted stone was in their custody, but the students deny they ever made any switch of stones. If the ancient monks did hide the real stone, they hid it well, as no other stone fitting the early description has ever been found.

So where is this elusive stone, the subject of much conjecture and search over the years? Could its existence be merely an elaborate myth perpetuated by romanticized belief? Many supposedly well-informed historical scholars think not; they continue to believe the legend and pore over ancient maps and writings with the hope of solving one of Scotland's greatest mysteries.

One interesting incident, possibly legend, has been related by the Earl of Mansfield, whose family has owned the lands around Scone Abbey for more than three hundred years. The story relates that sometime around 1705 to 1720, a young farm helper and his friend were wandering over Dunsinane Hill, site of King Macbeth's castle, after a violent storm. It seems torrential rain had caused a landslide, resulting in the exposure of a fissure that seemed to penetrate deep into the hillside. The two friends procured some form of lighted torch and returned to explore the fissure. Legend has it that some way into the narrow opening, they came upon a small subterranean chamber, and there in one corner they saw a slab of what seemed to be a rectangular granite rock supported by short, roughly hewn stone legs. With no other evidence of buried treasure, the two young men, not knowing the possible importance of their find, returned home and did not talk about their discovery.

A few years later, one of the now much-older friends became aware of some secret and secluded happenings at Scone Abbey carried out by the then-resident monks before King Edward's arrival. He heard the monks had placed a similar-sized stone, taken from the Annety burn, as a substitute for the real stone, and before the English arrived had hidden the original stone somewhere in the local area. After hearing this legend, the man hurried back to Dunsinane Hill, but whether his memory was at fault regarding the site of the landslide or whether the passage of time had obliterated the fissure with another landslide, he was unable to relocate the opening in the hillside.

Now, a few years after devolution, the Scottish nation has voted for and gained total independence from the United Kingdom government located at Westminster in London. The new Scottish government is committed to appointing a head of state similar to that presently presiding over the remains of the United Kingdom government, namely a monarch. This monarch, descended from King Robert the Bruce, Scotland's legendary hero king, will, in keeping with ancient tradition, be crowned sitting upon the Coronation Stone, that stone relocated from Edinburgh Castle to Scone Abbey for the ceremony. How much more meaningful would that crowning become if the ceremony were carried out not only using time-honored tradition but also using the original Stone of Destiny?

The Main Characters

Three unrelated native Scots—Tracy Dunbar, a Royal Navy fighter pilot operating from her ship in the South China Sea; Alan Stewart, a banker with part-time Auxiliary Marine police inspector duties in Hong Kong; and Grant Sinclair, an almost-destitute professional golfer in China—each receive separate and initially apparently unrelated "signs." These are received in the form of ancient tokens or coins. These three objects, when correlated by retired Edinburgh University archaeology professor Angus Gillespie and his assistant Elizabeth, bring all five people together in a common cause.

Angus had spent a lifetime studying the mystery of the Stone of Destiny, regrettably without much success. Now, with the help of Tracy, Alan, and Grant, his interest is greatly renewed. From medieval Christian chapels to the Buddhist temples of Hong Kong, and after the exhumation of an ancient king, Angus and his enthusiastic helpers must decipher clues they hope will solve one of the greatest mysteries in Scottish history—finding the hidden and much sought-after location of the true Stone of Destiny.

Glossary

Abin	Above
Auld	Old
Aw	All
Aye	Yes
Braw	Good
Burn	Small stream
Byre	Cowshed
Choug	Tough
Dinna	Do not
Ein	Eye
Fairmar	Farmer
Fit	What
Ga'in	Going
Gee	Give
Jist	Just
Kin	Family
Kirk	Church
Lavvy	Toilet
Loch	Lake
Loon	Young boy
Noo	Now
O'er	Over
Onny	Any
Peat	Compacted organic debris
Puckle	Many
Quinee	Young girl
Spate	High/flood water
Torch	Flashlight
Troot	Trout

Contents

Chapter 1

THREE PECULIAR TOKENS

Lieutenant Tracy Dunbar, (P) Royal Navy

Situation: 3,000 feet above the South China Sea

Few young children ever achieve their high ambitions and unrealistic dreams, but that was not the case for Tracy Dunbar. Born and raised as a single child in the central highlands of Scotland, she had far exceeded her own ambitions and expectations. She had completed four years mechanical engineering training at the Royal Navy's engineering school and a further year of on-the-job training at sea as a mechanical engineer. A fine career lay ahead in the weapons and weapon control system specialization, certainly more than twenty-two years pension qualifying service, but her ambition to become a military pilot had remained foremost in her mind. This she had achieved some four years ago, thanks to a change in naval training policy.

That change, namely accepting suitably qualified women into the Royal Navy's fixed-wing pilot training program, was considered quite revolutionary by many old seadogs, even though some WRENS (*Women's Royal Navy Service*) had been serving at sea for some time.

"Flying is different," the older pilots insisted, but they could not quantify the reasons for that view. It seemed to them, just "not quite the correct thing" to do.

Tracy had grasped what she considered a heaven-sent opportunity with both hands. She had successfully completed training against high odds and much male skepticism and now found herself at three thousand feet above the South China Sea. She anxiously awaited recovery back on board the aircraft carrier HMS *Ark Royal* as it ploughed through the darkening seas far below.

Flying her sleek, powerful twin-engine jet fighter in a holding circuit ahead of the ship, Tracy could not help but notice the threatening dark clouds laced with lightning lurking close by. Dusk had passed, day had quickly become night, and shortly a demanding night deck landing loomed ahead. Tracy Dunbar tried to settle again, calm her racing mind, and concentrate once more on the ever-increasing demand of the intimidating task ahead. She felt herself as being part of the twin-engine jet fighter strapped to her shoulders, waist, and thighs and took comfort from the knowledge that she was sitting on one of Martin Baker's most modern, safe, and reliable ejection seats.

She had already made two approaches to the angled deck of HMS *Ark Royal* within the past twenty minutes, but each approach had been waved off before Tracy could complete the final descent starting one mile astern of the ship. Tracy reasoned some non-communicated complication during the recovery phase of the two aircraft ahead was presumably the reason for the two wave-offs; not an unusual event.

Now, having been airborne at a low level and burning fuel at an extraordinary rate for many more minutes than expected from the mission plan, the aircraft was too low on fuel to divert safely ashore to the nearest airfield. Passing time was quickly burning up the Sea Vixen's remaining usable fuel, already at an alarmingly low level. To return safely on board, it was imperative for Tracy to make an accurate and steady approach, taking the arrestor hook of her sleek Sea Vixen into the waiting aircraft arrestor wires at precisely the calculated hook-on speed, 148 knots, nothing much more and certainly nothing less. Failing to hook on could mean climbing ahead, leveling off ahead of the ship at two thousand feet, and carrying out an ordered and premeditated twin ejection. Everything depended on the aircraft fuel situation.

The ejection, if required, would be done in tandem with her navigator, Kenny "Jock" Adams. Kenny's seat was only a few feet away but slightly below and to Tracy's right. He sat facing the weapons system attack and intercept radar screen, his rugged features lit by the screen's fluorescent glow. Kenny's crew position, commonly called the "coal hole," offered no forward vision other than a view of Tracy's legs working the aircraft rudders and part of the main blind flying instrument panel. A ten-inch-square window above and to his right gave some limited vision of the darkening tropical sky.

Lieutenant Tracy Elizabeth Dunbar had been making quite a name for herself in recent years. Tracy had, through great perseverance, skill, and dogged determination, become the Royal Navy's second-ever female fighter pilot, qualified for both day and night deck landings. She was currently attached to 892 Fleet Arm Squadron, operating from the aging aircraft carrier HMS *Ark Royal* presently completing her last Far East detachment operating in the South China Sea, some two hundred miles southeast of Hong Kong.

Thus qualified, Tracy had joined an exclusive "aviation club." She had achieved qualifications most aviators worldwide, military and civil, recognized as the pinnacle of piloting excellence. Most pilots viewed attainment of this standard with justified awe and envy. Tracy not only flew one of the Fleet Air Arm's most potent—yet potentially most unforgiving—jet fighters, the twin-jet Sea Vixen MK 2; she also carried the hopes and aspirations of many female pilots. All wished to emulate her spectacular success in a historically exclusive male order of excellence.

Many Fleet Air Arm pilots, especially those "old and bold" naval aviators of years gone by, were very much against female intrusion into their traditional dynasty. However, the younger, more modern pilots were certainly mindful of the ever-rising clamor for acceptance of gender equality. This equality, not only in remuneration and qualification, was seen to open up opportunity for women to achieve these very highest of qualifications previously only open to male navy pilots. The younger pilots openly supported Tracy and her aspiring followers.

The support from these younger navy pilots was very much against the stated views of the old and sometimes "not so bold" brigade and encouraged every opportunity be given to the "fairer sex." They were prepared to wait and watch. They made sure equal standards were applied to all aspects of training, regardless of gender, and so generally supported the female cause. If women could reach the highest standards of piloting, their answer was, *Why not?* However, underlying these thoughts of acceptance was always a sense of insecurity accompanying the threat of a competing new life order. Those barely out-of-their-teens pilots, however, seemed to take the view of an old adage; the proof of the pudding should be in the eating—and hopefully no one would get hurt in demonstrating so.

Some senior officers voiced their opinion those junior pilots were being naive, and this attitude had been tragically reinforced by a recent disastrous accident. Only three weeks before, operating from the sister aircraft carrier HMS *Eagle*, the navy's first female fighter pilot, Lieutenant Jane Randolph Smith, and her observer had both perished during a day approach, stalling into the sea just short of touchdown. Regrettably, the film of her approach and the taped communications pointed to the cause of the accident being Jane's fixation to land on board at all costs after two missed landings, what navy pilots called "bolters." Her fatal final approach was too tight, too slow, and too far below the required three-degree glide path that even the application of full power was insufficient to prevent the self-initiated super-stall situation. No ejection sequence was initiated, and all perished in the ensuing fireball as she, her crew, and the Sea Vixen slammed into the ship's churning wake.

A few anxious minutes passed, allowing the gravity of Tracy and Kenny's increasingly tenuous situation to sink into both of their minds.

"Not quite what we've been training for these past few months!" said Kenny over the aircraft's internal intercom.

"Not quite, Kenny, but we can do this. Just keep a close eye on my instruments. Tonight's weather is perfect for disorientation. Jab my right leg if things seem to be going haywire."

Kenny, sitting below in the coal hole, had a good view of the pilot's instrument panel. As a former pilot of some 350 hours' experience, he knew all about the disorientation problems even the finest pilots experienced and dreaded, especially at night.

"Go through your ejection procedure now," Tracy added. "We just might be out of here in a hurry somewhere down the line."

"Roger that," was Kenny's laconic reply.

"Vixen three," crackled the radio, "this is approach control. Call ready for recovery and vectoring to final talk down."

"Vixen three ready, now heading north," Tracy replied.

"Roger, Vixen three. Turn right heading east and descend to two thousand feet. Call level."

Throttling back, turning right, and commencing the standard-rate descent, Tracy soon called, "Vixen three leveling two thousand, heading east."

"Roger, Vixen three," answered the controller. "Turn onto one hundred eighty-five degrees, slow to final approach speed, and carry out landing actions—call complete."

Tracy now felt more comfortable. She had maneuvered the aircraft with skill and accuracy to this point, and all was standard and going well. However, the red light blinking next to the fuel gauges constantly reminded her of the urgency of the situation. She tried to ignore the warning light, leaving it out of her visual scan of the instruments, but it was always there. She thought about covering the flashing warning light up with tape, but that would take time and possibly break her concentration.

I can deal with this, she thought to herself.

Tracy reasoned that hundreds of thousands of pounds had been spent on getting her trained to deal with situations such as this, and at the moment the problem was really quite minor. However, the situation would dramatically change for the worse if there was yet another delay.

"Airbrakes in, undercarriage down, arrestor hook down, canopy locked and closed. Sufficient fuel! No instrument warnings . . ." These memorized checks and a few others Tracy called out to herself. *No time to worry about fuel now*, she thought and transmitted, "Vixen three approach checks complete; four green lights." (Green lights indicate the three wheels and the arrestor hook are down and locked.)

"Roger, Vixen three. Continue heading one hundred eighty-eight degrees and stand by for final controller."

Tracy acknowledged and took a last brief look ahead into the pitch-black night. There were no aircraft carrier lights in sight, but there were many fishing boats' lights that could be confused with low rising stars just appearing above the horizon.

Tracy took a deep breath, trying to control her mild hyperventilation but still hearing her fast-beating heart. "You okay, Kenny?" she asked. "Here we go."

"Just fine, Trace," was the calm and reassuring reply. "Hang in there; we've got this landing cracked. This will be easy after that wardroom rugby game the other night. What a bummer losing to those yobs from *Eagle*!"

Tracy summoned a wry smile inside the tightly clamped oxygen mask that covered all but her light blue eyes. She was fortunate to have Kenny by her side, bringing confidence, optimism, and some frivolity to the situation.

"Vixen three, this is your final controller; acknowledge."

Tracy knew that distinctive voice, and her confidence soared and then called, "Vixen three loud and clear. Is that you, Don?"

"Yup, Tracy, you can't run away tonight."

Tracy exhaled a short sigh of relief. "What's the trouble on board?" she inquired.

"Bits and pieces, bits and pieces," came back the melodious reply, sung to the tune of the popular Dave Clark Five hit song of the time.

Tracy smiled again, her spirits lifting some more.

"That's a good one," remarked Kenny.

"I wonder how long Don's been waiting for the opportunity to project his 'dull wit' on us poor, innocent, trusting aviators. He owes us a few beers later tonight."

Tracy had a fleeting memory of recent nights spent with Don in Singapore, Hong Kong, and Penang. They were somewhat hazy memories—memories dimmed by a few strong alcoholic drinks after sharing a full bottle of Tracy's favorite Merlot during dinner before retiring to bed in a local hotel. She resisted her own desires at first, but then the urge and pent-up passion of neglected hormones could not be restrained. They exhausted themselves with what seemed like hours of passionate lovemaking, but in reality those "hours" were more likely measurable in minutes. However, nobody else knew, and they often exchanged covert smiles in passing at the bar or dining table in the wardroom, the officers' dining and recreation area.

"Vixen three, you are approaching the glide slope . . . Now on the glide slope. Commence descent to maintain a three-degree glide slope approach. Acknowledge."

"Vixen three roger," acknowledged Tracy.

"Roger, Vixen three," was Don's professional, clear, and reassuring reply. "Do not acknowledge further instructions. You are now three miles from touchdown; you should be passing nine hundred feet . . . . Slightly left of the center line; correct three degrees right, steer one hundred ninety-one degrees . . . . Good steady approach, slightly above the glide slope; increase your rate of descent . . . . Now at two miles; you should be passing six hundred feet. The aircraft ahead is just about to touch down. Wind over the deck is twenty-six knots . . . . You are clear to land; acknowledge."

"Vixen three cleared to land," Tracy replied confidently.

"On the center line, one and a half miles from touchdown," Don continued. "Passing one mile and though three hundred feet, look ahead, call on sight, and acknowledge."

Tracy looked up and with relief, called, "Vixen 3, on sight."

She had made it. From here on it would be only seconds before she would feel the restraining jolt of the arrestor wire and the consequent need to throttle back from the full power setting she would apply upon feeling the violent jolt of landing.

Suddenly there was a blinding fireball only half a mile ahead. Large pieces of aircraft floated upward above the illuminated deck. Urgent calls flooded the radio, with screams of, *"Crash on deck! Crash on deck! Power, power, over-shoot!"* Bright red wave-off lights flashed, and a red rocket soared upward from beside the port projector sight into the confused sky. Tracy froze for a second.

"Power, power, add power," came Kenny's voice. When she did not respond, he bellowed, "Put the bloody power on!"

Tracy abruptly snapped out of her trance and responded with application of full power, pitched the aircraft up into a climb, and passed slightly above and to the left of the dying fireball. What had happened? Had Vixen 2 experienced a catastrophic ramp strike? Surely not, but in her heart Tracy knew that was the case. Had she lost yet another two friends on the same night that she would fight for her own and Kenny's life? Things were certainly not as expected, and oblivion might still lie ahead.

"Vixen three, I see you have overshot your approach. Climb straight ahead, clean up, and enter a left-hand hold two miles ahead," came Don's instructions. Somehow Don's steady voice calmed the situation, and Tracy responded.

"Vixen three roger," she answered, turning the aircraft toward the assigned waiting position.

Time seemed to stand still; even the silence seemed loud, and then an unfamiliar voice came over the radio.

"Vixen three, this is flight control." Tracy realized the ship's senior flying control officer had been brought in. "What is your fuel state?"

"Very low, five hundred pounds each side at the very most," replied Tracy. She knew the little remaining fuel was being gobbled up far too quickly even with the aircraft throttles backed off to barely maintain flying speed. Only three to four minutes remained before one or both jet engines flamed out.

"Didn't expect to make a Martin Baker let-down tonight," quipped Kenny, referring to the ejector seats both he and Tracy were strapped into.

"No, not quite," was Tracy's somber reply. "I wonder when Fly-co will give us the nod to leave our trusty steed."

The question was soon answered.

"Vixen 3, you are to fly one hundred eighty degrees on completion of your next turn. When on that heading and two miles ahead of the ship, you and your crew are to complete a premeditated ejection. This is an order. Acknowledge."

Fly-co.'s voice seemed stern, but some anxiousness broke through. Although there had been many successful ejections from naval aircraft, this one was at night, and sometimes things went horribly wrong.

"Fly-co, this is Vixen three. Roger your last."

Tracy pushed her right arm out in front of Kenny with her thumb up. "Got that, Kenny?"

"Yup," was his now less-than-steady reply. "Let's get on with it. Just give me the word and I'll be gone."

"Visor down, seat fully down, tighten shoulder and lap straps, locate one of the two firing handles with one hand, and trim the aircraft for level flight," Tracy called out over the intercom. "Set to go, Kenny?"

Kenny raised his left hand, thumb up, well within Tracy's view, and said, "Affirmative. Good luck; see you in the bar later." He then went back to making sure he had stowed all loose gear in the coal hole. By this time, a couple of minutes had passed and Tracy had maneuvered the aircraft to where she had been directed.

"Vixen three in position," she called, realizing it was going to be her last transmission from her beloved aircraft now doomed to a watery grave.

"Vixen three, eject, eject, eject," came the command order from Fly-co. "Do not acknowledge."

"Go, Kenny, go." On Tracy's call, Kenny pulled hard up on the ejection seat firing handle between his knees.

A loud bang from the exploding seat firing cartridge followed almost immediately, and the coal hole frangible hatch shattered. There was the roar of a 250-knot wind rushing into the open coal hole and Kenny was gone, experiencing fifty times the force of gravity for a tenth of a second as his tensed body and seat were thrust up and out to the right. But all was not well; in fact, all was dramatically wrong. Out of the corner of her impaired vision, Tracy gasped with horror and fear for Kenny's life. She could see Kenny's feet flailing in the wind blast; they seemed like a doll's broken legs attached to a tangled mass above. Somehow the small drogue parachute that should have opened to stabilize Kenny's main parachute had not deployed correctly. The drogue and the attached tightly woven silk parachute cords were now firmly wound around the protruding ejection seat firing barrel and Kenny. Kenny's ejection seat had left the aircraft, but somehow Kenny had separated early from his seat and still remained attached to the aircraft fuselage. The strong white nylon cords that should be supporting him underneath his parachute canopy were now tangled around his flailing body and firmly holding him half out of the coal hole.

Tracy froze for a second, delaying her own ejection, and called, "Fly-co, crew ejection is incomplete. Lieutenant Adams is partially out of the aircraft being buffeted by air blast; pass instructions."

"Invert and push negative gravity-force," Fly-co replied after a few seconds.

The wind blast noise was overwhelming. Tracy had never even dreamed of such a situation; this was certainly not in any training or emergency procedure manual.

Tracy inverted the aircraft and pushed forward on the control column, imposing high negative gravity upon the aircraft, hoping Kenny would be forced out and free from his restrained position. After two attempts, Kenny did not release. As Tracy leveled the aircraft after the second attempt, the starboard engine started to wind down, and multiple red warning lights lit up on the emergency warning panel caused by fuel starvation to the starboard engine.

Knowing she would lose all hydraulics when the port engine failed, which would also mean losing control of the hydraulic-operated control surfaces, Tracy yet again inverted the aircraft, trying to push Kenny out with negative force, but once again to no avail. With no useable fuel remaining, the port engine also started to wind down; now all hope of helping Kenny was gone. Tracy had visions of Kenny's wife, Kate, and their three children, Angus, Victoria, and young Martin, bereft of husband and father, and it was all her fault. How could she ever face the family again? How could she ever have drinks and dinner at their old Tudor cottage near the Squadron Headquarters at Yeovilton in west England? Why was the good Lord letting this happen?

Again the words, "Eject, eject, eject!" echoed through her helmet radio receiver, and as the aircraft hit the sea, she summoned up all her strength and pulled up hard on the ejection seat secondary firing handle between her knees. With a violent bang and an even more violent upward force, Tracy smashed though the heavy cockpit canopy, automatically separated from her ejection seat, hit the water, and was immediately covered by the immense swell of water from her aircraft's impact. She lost consciousness.

"Aircraft impact zone in sight."

The call was from Lieutenant Jeremy Nichols, pilot of the Plane Guard One search-and-rescue helicopter as he vectored with all haste toward Vixen 3's impact area and saw a raging white sea ahead.

"Any survivors?" called Fly-co.

"None in sight," replied Plane Guard One.

"Boss, I see one orange Mae West life jacket, right fifteen degrees, four hundred yards," called Leading Air Crewman Dave Jones, the helicopter rescue winch man and diver, as he anxiously scanned the water.

Tracy was recovered into the helicopter by tandem lift. Dave had lowered himself over Tracy's limp body, circled the spare lifting strop around her, and with the help of Jeremy's perfect hovering, she was safely winched up into the rescue helicopter cabin.

Tracy had experienced severe lacerations to her upper face as her helmet visor slammed down under the g-force of ejection; one arm was broken in three places when she hit the shattered canopy debris, and her right foot hung limp with multiple fractures caused by hitting the cockpit front cowling upon exit. Tracy had survived, and within an hour had been air-ferried by one of the Marine Commando longer-range Wessex 5 helicopters to the British Military Hospital in Hong Kong.

Two days later, a short memorial service for Lieutenant Kenny Adams was held on the quarterdeck of *Ark Royal,* followed by a traditional symbolic burial at sea. Kenny's body was never recovered; he lay entombed attached to Sea Vixen XG 435 some 350 feet below in the warm, tropical waters of the South China Sea.

Two weeks later, Tracy was able to sit up in bed. She was on her way to a full recovery, but her mind was still overloaded with the horrendous events that had culminated in the loss of her dear friend and fellow airman, Kenny Adams.

"Can I come in, ma'am?" called the gentle, low voice of Leading Seaman Dave Jones as he peered around the door into Tracy's private room.

Tracy recognized Dave's voice before seeing his face, her vision still not quite back to normal.

"Nice to see you again—a bit less traumatic than last time," she replied.

"Very true, ma'am," said Dave. "I have something for you. Can you see okay?"

"Not so good, but not so bad either," Tracy answered. "What do you have there?"

Dave fumbled in his deep right-hand trouser pocket and eventually produced the mangled remains of Tracy's service-issue aircrew watch.

"I just thought you'd like to have this. You can say it was lost during your accident and get another from flight safety stores once you gain medical clearance to start flying again."

Tracy was not sure she wished to have such a personal reminder of that night two weeks ago. But Dave had made a special effort to get the watch for her, a thing he had done before after another accident for another pilot. He had made a special trip to see her, and—well, what the heck? She accepted the watch and laid it alongside her wallet on the bedside table. Dave stayed a few more awkward minutes. It was difficult to not mention Kenny, and he did not really know how to handle what could easily become an emotional and guilt-ridden situation. He stood up from the visitor's chair, said a fond good-bye, and closed the door quietly behind him.

Tracy's recovery lasted another four weeks before she was cleared to fly back to England, commence medical leave, and retake the medical "fit for duty" examinations a month later. She had looked at her watch many times, knowing that nothing else remained that had been with her throughout the whole horrendous incident. She picked up the watch with now-trembling fingers. The watch had stopped at 10:51 p.m., the moment of impact. A flashing, nervous reaction made her fingers loose, and her watch clattered to the floor.

"Damn, I must get over this," she thought aloud and bent down to pick up the mangled watch to inspect the extra damage caused by its impact with the gleaming tiled floor. She noticed the back casing had partially detached and now hung loose from one side. Something gleamed inside.

While Tracy was trying to gently lever open the cover, it swung part open to reveal a strange-looking bronze-colored object—a coin. A gentle pull and the coin soon lay flat and gleaming in the palm of her hand. Strange it certainly was: an eye engraved within a triangle on one side and odd-looking symbols around the outer edge on the other. Tracy had seen her father's Masonic apron a number of times before she joined the navy, usually while he was gathering his Scottish Rite regalia before attending the local lodge meetings. The markings on the coin reminded her of similar markings embroidered onto the front of his Masonic apron; but what did this all mean? Where did this coin come from, and why had it been placed inside her aircrew watch?

She gazed at it with wonder and curiosity, thinking about its meaning and trying to form any symbolic link with her life or family history. Carefully she placed the coin into an inner pocket of her purse, never dreaming the coin was going to change her life forever.

Senior Auxiliary Marine Police Inspector Alan Lyle Stewart

Situation: Mirs Bay, Hong Kong

In the mid—to late 1980s, tens of thousands of illegal immigrants entered the British Crown Colony of Hong Kong. Many were caught by the border-patrolling armed services, the Hong Kong Land and Marine Police, and the associated auxiliary divisions of each service. A high percentage of those captured and returned to the custody of the Mainland China Administration and the PLA (People's Liberation Army, the Chinese police) were captured yet again trying to cross the border only a few months later.

Life had become an abomination for those not born into the "Great Leap Forward" regime of Chairman Mao. Many of those illegals—the more democratic and entrepreneurial-minded Chinese—yearned to join family members who had escaped to Hong Kong during the late 1940s, before the Communist regime took over the reins of oppressive government. The expanse of Mirs Bay, bordering mainland China to the north and west and the Hong Kong New Territories to the south, proved an inviting crossing point, with the border dividing the bay. The Chinese Navy and the Royal Hong Kong Marine Police carried out twenty-four-hour patrols along the border but concentrated their efforts at illegal immigrant control in Mirs Bay. However, the patrol boats were largely ineffective in turning back or picking up the masses of illegals. Many thousands of desperate mainland Chinese risked their lives crossing the rough and dangerous waterway mostly under the cover of darkness. The patrols stemmed but a trickle of the human tide.

Auxiliary Marine Police Inspector Alan Stewart was in command of the forty-eight-foot Marine Police Launch Alpha 5, currently heading north. A local Chinese and Indian crew, two sergeants and three seamen, were on board as they headed away from the shimmering lights of Victoria Peak towering above the bustling harbor. They had left the Marine Police Headquarters at Tsim Sa Tsui on the Kowloon side of Hong Kong Harbor about thirty minutes before dusk, but night had descended like a great dark blanket, and the darkness of Mirs Bay lay five nautical miles ahead.

Alan grinned as he remembered an experienced local police officer commenting, "Nothing good comes out after dark!" What a thought to start this night patrol of over ten hours. However, so far he had carried out more than thirty patrols at night without any really bad experiences. He was sure tonight would prove to be more of the same.

Alan Stewart was the second son of Ian and Wilma Stewart. He was born in the Cottage Maternity Home near the center of Roslin, a small town of two thousand or so people, located a few miles southwest of the Scottish capital city of Edinburgh. Alan had a very happy and active childhood roaming the nearby Pentland Hills and fishing the fast-running streams that tumbled down through the valleys. He and his elder brother, James, attended the local primary and secondary schools, both only minutes from their parents' stone Victorian home.

Alan's father, the local bank manager, had put high priority on his sons' education—but Alan, keen to contribute to the family coffers, decided to come up the hard way by leaving school at fifteen years of age. He completed evening classes while working in the nearby wool mill and was awarded his diploma in international banking after five years of tenacious study. The local Midland Bank offered him a teller's position, which he readily accepted. After some twelve years working in various banking positions in and around Edinburgh, Alan was eventually selected for a junior bank manager position. Very fortunately, after a few years in junior manager positions, he was appointed manager to the Linton Bank shortly after his father's retirement from the same position.

Bank managers were considered pillars of local society, along with school headmasters and doctors, and it was not unusual for all to be members of the local Masonic Order, a singularly Scottish trait. Alan being a Lewis, the son of a Mason, had been offered the opportunity to join, but with regret he declined. Having seen his father's deep involvement in the local order, he indicated he did not have the commitment required at this stage of his personal life and said he could not devote the many hours required to become an active, attending member. However, he did promise his father he would join one of the many registered Scottish Rite Masonic Lodges sometime in the future.

Rosslyn Chapel, of *The Da Vinci Code* and Knights Templar fame, was situated only a few miles from Linton close by the village of Roslin, but it had not been restored to its former glory during Alan's youth. When he was young, many of the local children played hide and seek and other popular games in the crumbling chapel. All Roslin children had an intimate knowledge of the chapel—but little did Alan dream that his familiarity with the chapel would become important to him in later life.

In the mid-1980s, the Midland Bank was acquired by the world-renowned Hong Kong and Shanghai Banking Corporation. Considering the business relationship Scotland had nurtured for almost one hundred years with Hong Kong, it was natural that some Scottish bank managers were posted to Hong Kong to gain international experience working in one of the world's premier financial centers. This meant working in the Hong Kong and Shanghai Bank's magnificent new headquarters located in the Victoria area of Hong Kong Island, bordering the magnificent harbor. Shortly after the amalgamation Alan had been posted to the Hong Kong head office, and it was there he had worked for the three years.

Many of the Europeans living and working in Hong Kong were traditionally obliged to complete some public service in addition to their normal everyday duties. Alan had always fancied himself as a naval officer. He completed a number of sailing courses and gained his power-boat operating certificate shortly after arriving in the colony. During his weekends away from banking duties, he often acted as master of the bank's powerful forty-eight-foot motor launch, a "gin palace," by most accounts; with this experience, it was natural for him to join the Royal Hong Kong Auxiliary Marine Police. After six months' training, attending instruction two evenings a week, Alan graduated from the marine police training school with the rank of inspector. Shortly after graduating, he was appointed to the Marine Police Illegal Immigrant Patrol Unit working alongside the full-time marine police, mostly during weekends.

Hong Kong is an enigma. How a peaceful, uncrowded place stays poor is difficult to explain. How a conflict-ridden, grossly overpopulated place with no natural resources gets rich is simple. The British colonial government formed Hong Kong into an economic miracle by doing nothing. Hong Kong is the best contemporary example of *laissez-faire* economics known to man. The *laissez-faire* economic theory holds that all sorts of doings should be allowed, and that government should interfere only to keep the peace, ensure legal rights, and protect property. The people of Hong Kong were free to do whatever they wanted, and what they wanted was to create a whirling pandemonium, crowded and striving—and the most fabulous city in the world. It is a metropolis of avenues too busy and broad to cross. It is a vertical city, rising eighteen hundred feet from the central district to Victoria Peak in less than a mile; it is so vertical that escalators run in place of sidewalks and neighborhoods are named by altitude. Hong Kong is a rich city, except where it is almighty poor; it is full of "poverty amidst plenty." Over the hilly terrain in dense traffic, men nonetheless drive their Turbo 911s. The S-class Mercedes is the Honda Civic of Hong Kong, and for the soccer mom set, a Rolls Royce and a driver is a mini-van.

Alan loved the new society he had been introduced to and certainly tried to live up to all its expectations.

"Contact right fifteen degrees, heading two hundred thirty degrees, speed sixteen knots," announced the anxious voice of Sergeant Milka Singh, the launch navigator that evening.

"Roger, sergeant," said Alan, leaning forward looking over at the plan view radar screen. "Do you think it's one of those bastard Chinese gunboats out of position?" he wondered aloud. "It must be, if I'm reading the range correctly; they're at least five miles over our side of the border."

"Could be," replied Sergeant Singh and added, "Shall I come starboard a little?"

Alan knew with the other boat heading 230 degrees on a steady bearing from Launch Alpha 5, he would be on the gunboat's port side. With the range closing, there was a risk of collision if he did not alter heading—and Alan knew that the gunboat had right of way according to the International Seamanship Rules of the Road.

"Starboard thirty degrees, reduce speed to ten knots, and keep good visual contact with the gunboat," ordered Alan.

The gunboat, only one mile on his port bow with the range closing quickly, seemed oblivious to Launch Alpha 5's position. Alan remembered stories about these gunboats running down illegals in the water when there were too many swimmers to pick up. That maneuver seemed their simple solution to part solving the immigration problem. Alan also remembered similar stories about Icelandic gunboats' participation in the "Cod War" of the late 1950s. Royal Navy frigates sent to enforce the twelve-mile international offshore boundaries were continually harassed by Icelandic gunboats, and some collisions had occurred. But these Chinese vessels were being deliberately aimed at the illegal swimmers; many Chinese illegals were mutilated and cut apart by the gunboats' propellers and left to become the prey of the ever-attendant circling thresher sharks' feeding frenzies. Alan decided to give all these sometimes-murderous gunboats a wide passing distance, and in so doing, he himself almost entered Mainland Chinese territorial waters.

"Mr. Stewart, sir! Typhoon signal number three has now been raised in Hong Kong Harbor," shouted Sergeant Au Kim Hung from inside his radio shack. Then he added, "Shall we make for Shatin Typhoon shelter or remain on patrol?"

Alan had been briefed by his operations officer three or four hours earlier about the impending arrival of Typhoon Charise. The early-season typhoon, churning through the warm waters of the South China Sea some two hundred miles southwest of Hong Kong, must have increased in speed, as Alan had not anticipated the typhoon warnings till early next morning. A decision had to be made—his decision—and there was not much time in which to make it. To call off his patrol meant returning to Shatin without having intercepted or apprehended any illegal immigrant swimmers. His crew would experience great loss of face in the eyes of the other launch crews if they returned empty-handed. Alan appreciated the situation—although he thought it more likely the crews were betting on the number of illegals picked up during each patrol. He decided to stay on patrol another hour.

"Time to head for Shatin," exclaimed Sergeant Hung after fifty minutes of boredom.

"Okay, head two hundred thirty-eight degrees and we're out of here," ordered Alan, somewhat disappointed at having to return to base. But he really did know the score, having only two months before experienced the fury of Typhoon Betty. It was, to say the least, frightening and not an experience to be repeated.

"Hey, boss," exclaimed Sergeant Singh. "Did you hear about the condom raft Alpha 3 intercepted the other night?"

"Yes I did," responded Alan. He added, "Quite a novel invention. Those mainland Chinese are very inventive, but I suppose anything goes if it gets the job done."

The mainland China administration had recently shown concern about the exploding population. They had issued an edict concerning the official Chinese family size: one child per married couple. To help enthusiastic couples curtail the birth rate, the government had mandated the use of condoms and had provided two a week for the use of sexually active couples, hoping the birth rate would be reduced. However, the inventive would-be immigrants had grasped this windfall with open hands. Rather than using them as reproductive suppressants, a few illegal swimmers had been picked out of the water using their past week's issue as blow-up water wings! Some three or four couples had joined forces and produced a few of the aforementioned condom rafts. They were not exactly a recognized seaworthy means of transport, but they were adequate for even the dark and dangerous Mirs Bay crossing if the wind was from a favorable direction.

Tonight there was such a wind, but the raft system seemed to have gone out of favor. They were a much larger and more compact target for the patrolling ships' close-range radar to detect. In the past month immigrants had been arriving as single persons using the condom method—as Alpha 5 would see that night.

"Radar contact low in the water ahead, three hundred yards," sang out Sergeant Au. After a moment, he added, "Now visual; two contacts in sight."

"Slow to five knots," ordered Alan. "Prepare to pick up two swimmers."

As the launch came alongside the two illegal swimmers, one put his hands above his head, and calling out a word of praise to Buddha—like a suicide bomber shouting, "Allah is great!"—the swimmer sank down into the deep, dark waters. He did not reappear.

Alan had seen this before. This illegal, seemingly of mature age, must have been carrying the wealth of his whole family on his person. Rather than letting himself be captured and the family wealth confiscated, he preferred to drown honorably. Such was the power of losing face among Cantonese families. This man could not face the consequences of failure and returning in disgrace to his optimistic family. Better for them to think he might have succeeded in joining relatives in Hong Kong rather than know he had failed—and with that failure, extinguish any hopes they all had of joining their family members over the border in Hong Kong.

"Quickly, get that second man on board!" ordered Alan. "Don't burst those wings, or he'll sink just like his pal."

"Okay, sir, we've got him," said Sergeant Singh as a boathook handled by one of the crew members was hooked into the swimmer's upper clothing.

"Steady now. Half astern, Sergeant Au, half astern," ordered Alan, and the launch came to a halt.

A minute or so later, the swimmer stood up straight before his captors. He was tall for a mainland Chinese. Alan thought maybe he was of Mongolian birth.

"Ask him where he's from, his name, and whether are there any other swimmers with him," ordered Alan.

"He does not speak any Cantonese," said Sergeant Au. "All he says is *Gwilow, gwilow, give to gwilow.*" Alan knew that *gwilow* was the Cantonese for "white man devil," or something similar. "I presume he wants to meet with you, sir," added Sergeant Au.

Alan stepped a few paces forward to see this swimmer more clearly. Certainly this young survivor with the shaved head who stood shivering on the deck seemed intent on meeting him. He held his clasped hand out toward Alan. Opening his clenched fist, he revealed what seemed to be a small coin. He uttered some unintelligible Mandarin, placed the coin in Alan's hand, and then quickly turned and dived overboard. No one could stop him, and he never reappeared.

"Wow!" exclaimed Alan. "I've never seen anything like that before!"

"What did he give you?" asked the sergeant.

Alan and Sergeant Au looked at the round, copper-colored, coin-like object.

Much ado about nothing, thought Alan. Slipping the "coin" into the breast pocket of his uniform jacket, he asked aloud, "What on earth could this all mean?"

Grant Sinclair, Professional Golfer

Situation: Mission Hills Golf Resort, Canton Province, China

The ability to hit a golf ball straight, long, and accurately has been a skill sought worldwide by young and old, rich and not so rich—and also by kings, queens, and presidents in almost every country in the world—for over four hundred years. Those who succeed can become sporting idols, multimillionaires, and respected role models for people of all ages, yet those who do not achieve these high stations in life can still enjoy the game long into old age. The game humbles not only the high and mighty but also those with the inflated egos who can come with other life successes in both business and other sports, no matter what level achieved.

Grant Sinclair had a golfing talent handed to him almost from birth. He was one of those gifted natural athletes who arrive on this earth from time to time with the ability to seemingly conquer all sports. Grant, however, had squandered those talents over the years from his youth to manhood, but at least was now playing at second, or more probably third-tier level, in his chosen sport—namely golf. It was a special invitation, and that alone brought him to Mission Hills to participate in the Canton Open, a fast-growing and respected event on the Asian Professional Golf circuit.

Grant was the only son of Andy Sinclair, the locally born professional at the not-so-well-known Panmure Golf Club. The Panmure course and club were only minutes from the world-renowned Carnoustie Open Championship course on the east coast of Scotland about twenty miles north of Dundee and thirty miles north of Edinburgh, as the crow flies. Grant had been singularly academically inept at school but good at all sports. Soccer, cricket, rugby, tennis, and even darts—to name but a few—came to him naturally. There are no sporting scholarships to colleges or universities in Scotland; one has to get into college on academic ability alone. This situation makes selection for entry into a university very competitive.

Grant had won a number of amateur golfing events within his local area. He was eventually picked to represent Scotland at sixteen years of age, which gained him his first amateur international honor, a remarkable achievement for someone at such a young age. But becoming a golf professional is not just about playing golf. Aspiring professionals have to compete in playing ability tournaments, attend the Professional Golfers Association players' school, pass business and golf-related subjects, and generally conduct themselves to the high standards required of that profession.

Grant could not see himself as a club professional like his much-respected father. Passing his exams could wait; he wanted to play on tour, *now*. However, it took Grant three attempts to pass the playing standards at qualifying school to gain his Professional Golfers Association playing card—and even then, it often took some good fortune, combined with exceptional play, to meet the required standards to earn his card.

Grant, being a native son of Scotland, the country where the game supposedly originated in the fifteenth century, seemed to have all the tools for the game, but it would be some time before those tools would come together—in fact, just over ten years.

The place where it all came together turned out to be in China at the Mission Hills Golf Resort, supposedly the best golf resort in the world. Stretched out there are fourteen signature-designed courses, another two full-sized practice courses, two driving ranges with attendant professional teachers, and a multitude of other impressive facilities: a massive clubhouse, three large swimming pools, many oversized professional golf shops, and a whole range of high-end, high-priced villas and condominiums bordering most of the courses' fairways. Golf had come to this part of mainland China in a big way.

But golf was not the only close connection between China and Scotland. For many years, the many poems and songs of Scotland's national bard, Robert Burns—most famous as the author of "Auld Lang Syne"—had been reproduced and studied in schools and colleges and universities. Burns was a renowned socialist, so it was natural that his works exalting the trials and tribulations of the "common working man" were popular government tools in China and Russia, both socialistic-minded countries, albeit embracing a dubious form of socialism called Communism.

Grant's father had joined the Masonic Order during midlife and enjoyed lodge work—as, indeed, was the case for Robert Burns some two hundred years before. Grant's father especially enjoyed administrating the many Masonic-funded charities of the time, and once he saw his son was hell-bent on going it alone into professional golf, he prevailed upon him to also join, and for good reason. Grant, being born a Lewis, was readily accepted into the order and soon realized the advantages of so doing. He became a member in good standing in word and in deed and attended lodge meetings regularly wherever he traveled.

Zetland Hall, located in the mid-levels of Victoria in Hong Kong, was used by a number of Masonic Lodges as their administration offices. Zetland Hall also had a magnificent temple within which the various lodge rituals and meetings were held on a monthly basis. Most lodges followed the Scottish rite, although others followed the English, Welsh, and Irish rites—but none of these had been long established in Hong Kong, where the Scottish expatriate had been predominate in setting up the early administration of the crown colony over one hundred years before. Each lodge had many Chinese members, from both Hong Kong and mainland China, and many other members from nearby countries, such as Taiwan and Japan.

Whenever playing tournaments in Hong Kong or staying there overnight, Grant always paid Zetland Hall a visit, seeking out fellow Scottish Rite members. He became so popular with these members, many of whom played golf and were members of the prestigious Royal Hong Kong Golf Club, that those members arranged for him to become an honorary member of the club. Of course, Grant gave golf lessons in kind to those members who were helping him through this difficult time during which he had shown so much promise but had produced mediocre success. As an honorary member, Grant was allowed to declare himself as "playing out of the Royal Hong Kong Golf Club," and so gained status and recognition that brought tournament sponsors' invitations to play in tournaments worldwide, a big personal accomplishment that eventually made for a good but not overly expensive lifestyle. However, life for Grant was soon to change—though not in a way he could have expected or even imagined.

A number of the Chinese members of Grant's mother lodge, namely Lodge Western Scotia, were also respected members of Mission Hills Golf Resort and Club. As sponsors of the Mission Hill Open Golf Tournament, they had the right to offer a "sponsor's exemption" to various players, meaning those players did not have to qualify to enter the tournament. Being offered a sponsor's exemption was a much sought-after privilege, and Grant was most honored to be awarded one. He was very keen to prove worthy of his friends' confidence in his playing ability.

But all was not going well. Grant had made minimal amounts of prize money, even though he had entered as many as forty tournaments every year since turning professional, and his sponsors were losing faith in his ability to ever break through. Grant's Hong Kong sponsors had indicated to him the Mission Hills Open would probably be the last tournament they would sponsor him to enter; enough was enough.

Now the pressure was really on. At thirty years of age, Grant had run out of funding, he had no stable lifestyle, he had recently split from his last love—a pretty Eurasian girl whose family were very much against Grant and his "wandering minstrel" lifestyle—and this latest ultimatum could very well mean an end to his somewhat haphazard career.

Many of the golf caddies employed at the Royal Hong Kong Golf Club were traditionally Hakka women, ever since the club's founding in 1882. It was not unnaturally the same case at Mission Hills, although Mission Hills was a much newer golfing destination. But there was one exception—Ah Ying. Hakka women, mainly from the southern province of Guangdong, were easily identified by their stature and dress. Almost all were less than five feet three inches tall, and all dressed in drab, dark-colored, loose-fitting two-piece garments and wore black wide-brimmed veiled hats for protection from mosquitoes and other flying insects.

Ah Ying was different. She was tall, almost six feet, and had facial features that more closely resembled the people of northern China and Mongolia. Despite her loose-fitting garments, it was obvious she had a slim but full-bosomed figure, and she walked as though she had been trained as a runway model. She was definitely a misfit, but even so—and despite speaking a Mandarin dialect quite different from the Cantonese of the Hakka women—she had better-than-average knowledge of the game of golf. This knowledge had been essential in getting her the caddie job at Mission Hills, but where it came from remained a complete mystery. There were no golf courses in northern China, and books describing the game were very few and far between. She spoke very little about her past and family; however, the Hakka people have a strong traditional sense of hospitality and friendship, and she was readily accepted into the Hakka women's lives.

Most successful touring golf professionals have their own professional caddie who travels with the player—"their" player—all over the world. These caddies are essential in providing knowledge of each course and advising their players on the type of shot to play, and the reading of all the greens when putting. Hakka caddies were delegated by their caddie master to players requiring a local caddie, and they were generally good at giving advice to players, albeit in very broken English, but made good use of their local knowledge of the courses and greens. In this respect too, Ah Ying was different. The caddie master allowed her to pick the player she wished to caddie for. Normally the Hakka women pulled a two-wheeled golf cart with the bag attached on top, and they generally positioned themselves a few paces behind their player during the round.

Ah Ying walked beside her golfer, the heavy bag slung over her erect shoulders. She paced out distances, gave easily understood and graceful hand signals when reading the greens, and generally contributed much-appreciated advice about distance and direction during play—again, all by hand signal and gesticulation. She would only from time to time say, *"Hoho"*—good—when the shot was to her satisfaction. She never commented when any shot played did not meet her approval.

Ah Ying picked Grant as her player for the Mission Hills tournament. The prize money was good, over $1.2 (US) million for the winner, down to $22,000 for the seventieth player. Only 70 players out of 162 qualified to play the final two rounds of the four-round tournament, depending on each player's first two scores. As Grant had gained sponsor's entry, he was one of the 162 starters, and once again his hopes were high as he teed off at 8:30 a.m. the first day. He had played two good practice rounds earlier in the week with the ever-attendant Ah Ying by his side.

He was drawn to Ah Ying; he liked her easygoing but attentive attitude and her obvious and extremely helpful knowledge of the course and its tricky greens—and he could not help but imagine what lay under her loose-fitting caddying suit, his name emblazed on the back.

Despite playing well, Lady Luck did not seem to be with Grant. Putts lipped out, he found his ball rolling to rest in divot holes a couple of times after great drives, and he only scored "level par" after sinking a monster putt on the last hole—a putt he knew was really his only good piece of luck during the whole round.

"If I hadn't had bad luck, I would have had no luck," he quipped to Ah Ying after the round. She seemed to smile in sympathy. "See you tomorrow at 1:30 p.m., here on the practice tee," he added.

"*Yut dime poon*," (1:30) answered Ah Ying, pointing to her battered old watch.

"*Joy geen*," (See ye) replied Grant in his almost non-existent Cantonese.

Grant had a few Glenmorangies—his favorite malt whisky—before retiring to bed. He could not get to sleep. His whole career depended on his score tomorrow, and he was fantasizing about Ah Ying! Of all the caddies available for hire, why her? He thought about his father and the "told you so" talk he was bound to endure if he gave up and returned home, cap in hand. He thought about what could have been, about the strange quirks of life he had endured, and about the loss of Alice, his latest female companion. He had come to admit that all his lady friends were really just convenient companions. His relationships seemed to be of the "ships that pass in the night" variety, and he had lied about being a very successful touring professional golfer—all of which was true except the "very successful" bit. Why lie? After all, everyone could read the tournament results the next day in national and local newspapers.

"I'm a sorry, sorry mess," he said out aloud, addressing his mirror image. "What have I done to deserve this? Nothing."

But actually *nothing* for twelve long years, he now realized, was the correct word as he pondered upon his dismal career.

"Tomorrow's going to be another day with Ah Ying by my side, maybe for the last time," he said out loud. But eventually he fell asleep, lost in thoughts of his desire for respect as a professional golfer—but mostly of his desire for Ah Ying.

The next day, the starter's voice rang out over the loudspeaker: "Ladies and gentlemen, this is the two-thirty afternoon players pairing. On the tee, Grant Sinclair from Panmure, representing the Hong Kong Golf Club. Play away please."

Grant took a nervous practice swing, followed by an average tee shot about two hundred and seventy yards down the right of the first fairway, but running into a shallow bunker.

Not again, thought Grant, inwardly complaining about another perfectly hit shot producing a poor result.

Each hole he played seemed to be uphill. He made some poor shots, but not that bad. However, his score was a poor two over par coming to the fifteenth hole—a masterful long par five with a dogleg right and deep bunkers about halfway to protect the right short approach to the green. The green was protected on both sides by deep pot bunkers and undulated some sixty-eight yards from front to rear. Grant found his ball lying quite well in the bunker but atop a slight rise in the sand.

"Well, that's a change," remarked Grant to Ah Ying. She gave him an unusual wry smile.

Now with a five wood, Grant proceeded to play one of his best-ever shots. The ball flew two hundred and thirty yards through the air, straight for the right of the green. It gave a skip and a bounce, but hit a sprinkler head on the bounce, and ran off the side into one of those pot bunkers.

"That's to be expected today, with my bloody luck," exclaimed Grant. "I might as well pick up and go home now." He glowered at Ah Ying as he spoke to himself.

Grant lowered himself into the bunker and immediately noticed some recent footprints beside where his ball lay. This he thought unusual. Normal practice required all footprints made by the players ahead to have been raked smooth by each player's caddie after clearing the bunker.

"Sand wedge, Ah Ying," he called out.

But Ah Ying already had the club in hand. She gave it to him but retreated only a few paces. Grant wondered why she was standing so much closer for this shot than the others; she usually positioned herself at least ten yards away to offer no distraction. It seemed she especially wanted to see this shot.

Women the world over are odd characters, even here in China. No consistency, thought Grant, and prepared for the task at hand, an almost impossible sand shot. *Anywhere on the green will do, never mind about close to the pin*, he told himself.

Beginning with a steep backswing, Grant changed the club's direction and brought the accelerating sand wedge down to strike just an inch or so behind the ball. At the moment of impact, a definite un-golf-like sound rang out, a sound of metal hitting metal, but the ball still flew up quickly—but not quick enough. It just caught the edge of the bunker, continued much lower and faster than intended across the green, hit the flagpole, and dropped into the hole. Grant stood amazed, Ah Ying smiled, and the few spectators watching Grant and his playing partner clapped respectfully, though without much enthusiasm.

"Good eagle," exclaimed Harry Devine, Grant's playing partner.

"Ho-ho," said Ah Ying—the first *ho-ho* she had uttered since the start, three and a half hours earlier.

Now Grant's luck changed and very much for the better. He birdied two of the last three holes and with a score of two under par qualified for the final two rounds over the next two days.

That afternoon, after telling Ah Ying the time to meet him the following day, he sat on the club veranda, contemplating his turn of good luck—and maybe fortune. After some time, he noticed Ah Ying out at the fifteenth green, where he had scored his eagle. She wandered around for some time in the area of the pot bunker he had played from. As he watched, she bent down, appeared to pick something up, and then headed back toward the caddies' quarters.

Maybe something she dropped, maybe something from my bag when she laid it on the ground before smoothing out the sand, thought Grant. *Maybe just plain anything, maybe a ritual for good luck, maybe a short prayer to her forbearers . . . Who knows? These Chinese have strange ways and habits.*

"Another Glenmorangie and water," Grant requested of a nearby waiter and turned his mind to other things, namely a rather nice young lady who had asked for his autograph after finishing his round. She stood at the entrance to the members' bar.

I might as well take advantage while the illusion lasts, mused Grant with half-hearted hope. But the young lady seemed more interested in getting other autographs, and thoughts of a possible liaison quickly rushed from his mind.

Being with her tonight would have really made my day, thought Grant as he headed upstairs to the club accommodation where he was staying that night.

As often observed in life, so too in sports competition; success often leads to more success. And so it was for Grant during the last two rounds of the Mission Hill tournament. He played his lifetime best golf; luck seemed at last to be on his side. Other competitors fell back, and Grant finished in a very respectable fifth place. Ah Ying had been exemplary in her advice and accepted her percentage of Grant's prize money with good grace and gratitude before fading from the scene like a ghost. Fifth prize, after Ah Ying's percentage, amounted to $380 thousand (US), to be paid into any bank of Grant's choice—tax-free. It was more than Grant had won during his whole professional career, an amount of money he had only dreamed about winning.

That evening, after a few celebratory drinks, Grant retired to his room upstairs, tired but elated and flushed with the happiness of success. He fell asleep, but the opening of his unlocked bedroom door about midnight wakened him and certainly caught his attention.

A tall, elegantly dressed woman stood framed in the light of the bright hallway. Closing the door, she moved toward his bed and motioned him to be silent by raising a finger to her mouth. Grant was now very much awake, all his senses recovered from his sleep as he gazed with wide eyes fixed steadily on the familiar figure before him—a figure now elegantly dressed, not the drab clothes he was used to seeing on Ah Ying. Could it truly be?

"Is that really you, Ah Ying?" asked Grant in an incredulous and almost inaudible voice.

"Yes, Grant," she replied in perfect English.

"Ah Ying, I am very confused; I cannot understand."

"No need to understand, Grant. Just know that I am here for you tonight; your inner thoughts of these past few days will be fulfilled. My journey is complete, but yours is just about to begin."

She started to undress and lay down beside Grant with all bared. He could now see all that he had imagined for the past six days. Ah Ying was no beginner in the art of satisfying "her player." Grant realized, as time went by, he had only been playing at lovemaking in previous relationships; it was he who now proved to be the apprentice.

The light from the rising sun streamed into Grant's eyes. He roused himself and looked around. Ah Ying was nowhere to be seen. There was no trace of her ever having been there; no trace of her sensuous perfume filled the morning air. Had it all been just a dream?

Yes, it was all a dream. A wonderful dream to finish a wonderful day, thought Grant. But just then something caught his eye: a coin or token of sorts laying on his bedside table. It was certainly not his, and beside it lay a written note.

Grant lifted the note and read the perfectly printed words.

This token lay beneath your ball in the fifteenth bunker. Your journey began then, as you struck that first blow to your destiny. Keep this special token; treasure its yet-to-be-revealed meaning, and return the good fortune that will surely follow.

Grant picked up the token with shaking hands. Yes, she had been there; she had shared herself with him. And now this message. What could it all possibly mean? Ah Ying had vanished from his life; would she ever reappear? Did she really even exist? And why the charade?

Turning the coin over and over in his hand, he stood, bemused. Was this strange coin—with an eye inside a triangle on one side and concentric rings of what he took to be some ancient alphabet engraved on the reverse—really going to control his destiny?

Chapter 2

THE BRAVEST HEART

February 1307

The king sat at the entrance to a small cave on the west coast of Scotland, staring into the embers of a fire that had sputtered out in the cold, driving rain.

"Where has all the promise gone, Sir James?" asked Robert Bruce, king of Scots.

"All is not lost, my liege," replied Sir James Douglas, the king's chief war lieutenant. "We are at the end of the beginning, not the beginning of the end." But he knew Robert Bruce had little to show for a kingdom that day.

"Sir James, even you cannot deny that English garrisons, as well as Scottish lords loyal to England's king, now occupy most of our lands. Civil war has pitted our clansmen against one another . . . Even our churchmen take sides, and now we ourselves have been excommunicated by the pope," replied a weary-voiced Robert, almost in tears of frustration. "Those cowardly servants of Edward have not only publicly hanged, beheaded, and mutilated three of my own brothers; they've also sentenced my sister Mary and the countess of Buchan to be locked in cages and hung from the walls of England's castles. My wife, my twelve-year-old daughter, and my other sister are all captives in the Tower of London," he continued, turning his head away in shame and humiliation.

"Surely our day will come," responded Sir James. "It certainly will with you leading us."

"Do you think the good Lord is with us?" asked Robert.

"Sire, we cannot—we *must not* lose heart! Our nation's future depends on us! We must continue, we must fight on, we must never give in!" responded Sir James.

No one in Scotland could have ever expected this heartbroken man would successfully evade Edward's armies, mold his small band of followers into an effective fighting force, and finally drive the English out of Scotland for all time. At this time it seemed King Robert's reign would never last until its second year, and there would never be an independent Scotland to rule over. A short revolt by a relatively minor landowner, William Wallace, kept alive the hopes of Scottish independence, but in 1305 a pro-English Scotsman had turned Wallace over to Edward, who had barbarously executed him.

Following Edward's reprisals against Scotland, only two major claimants remained to openly contest the Scottish throne—namely Robert Bruce and John Comyn. Both had escaped Edward's vengeance by signing oaths of allegiance to him, but both eventually defied the English king by pressing their own legitimate claims to the Scottish crown.

"When I met with Comyn in Greyfriers Kirk last February, I should not have argued with him," said Robert. "We should have talked more about succession to the crown. Instead of losing my temper, we should have settled things in a gentlemanly manner. I should never have drawn my dagger and killed him on the steps of the kirk; the Lord will never forgive me for defiling his holy house. He is making me pay dearly. Is there no salvation, no sign I can take heart from, no guiding light of hope to follow?"

"Sire, you did act hastily, going to Scone for your coronation so soon after Comyn's death," replied Sir James. "But you had to do what was needed. John Comyn was no Robert the Bruce. The fact that your coronation was still held and recognized without sitting upon the Stone of Destiny is a grand testimony to what your loyal servants needed and dearly wished for."

"Aye, and I hope Edward is happy with the stone he carried off," added King Robert, with a half-smile.

"I hear the monks replaced the real stone with a stone similar in size and weight that had been used as a cesspit cover. The English kings and queens will sit upon a lavvy pot at all their future coronations! A finer sight I cannot imagine, if the story holds true," said Sir James, smiling as he imagined all the English monarchs being crowned sitting on "their convenience"—so to speak!

"Yes, Sir James, you are correct. While many question the manner in which I gained the crown, immediate action had to be taken to stop the fragmentation of Scotland. You remember the greed, avarice, and fear that enticed so many of our fine nobles into signing oaths of allegiance to Edward, just as we two did, while those who wanted to remain free had little hope."

"But sire, we had great success to begin with. Edward's armies were not as mobile as ours in the beginning, and it was only by sheer weight of numbers they defeated us at Methven and Dalry," commented Sir James.

"Aye, Sir James, you speak the truth. What now? We have lost many men after they lost faith in our cause. Now we are here hiding like rats in a sewer."

A silence descended on the two patriots. Neither spoke for an hour or so. Each man, deep in his own thoughts, forgot to tend to the fire, and it finally sputtered out, just as Bruce's fine efforts against the English King Edward had done a few weeks before.

The evening wore on, becoming even more chilly and wet as night set in. However, Robert's attention was drawn to the antics of a spider at the mouth of the cave. At last he spoke to Sir James.

"See yon spider trying to spin its web across the entrance to this cave?" said Robert to his trusted friend.

"Aye, I see it. I've been watching it for some time now," replied Sir James. "It really is tenacious and focused on the task."

Robert went on. "Each time the spider has tried to spin a strand, the wind and rain have broken it down. But I observed that on the seventh try, the strand held, and the spider completed the web."

"Well, sire, we have tried six times to kick out Edward and his cronies, and each time we have failed. Is the spider's success at its seventh attempt a good omen, a sign from God to try again? We must surely heed this sign; we must try again!"

In admiration of the spider's persistence, Bruce determined he would not give up. Try again he did—and this time his actions resulted in spectacular success.

Bruce's small army could not meet the English in pitched battle, but he knew he could not stay on the run and hope to rally his people. Developing a plan that was foreign to medieval concepts of warfare, Bruce adapted the raiding skills of the fleet-footed and lightly armed Highlanders loaned to him by Angus Oag, Lord of the Isles. He turned these Gaelic-speaking tribesmen into a deadly guerrilla force who could travel fast and strike quickly. With each small victory, more supporters came to his aid. Few Scots wanted a foreigner on their throne, and Bruce offered the only alternative.

Robert Bruce led by example, and his courage and daring in battle became legendary. His followers admired the way he fought alongside his men, sharing their meager rations and their difficult way of life. Success bred success, and a spectacular victory over the mighty English army was soon to be his.

"Who is this upstart Bruce who harasses our men in Scotland?" demanded King Edward of his warlords and knights. "Who is this man who dares challenge my God-given rights? How dare he pronounce himself king of Scots, and by whose authority? Have I not claimed their Stone of Destiny to be my own? I am their Lord Paramount! The Scots are all my subjects and beholden to my word! I may be a sick man, but I will raise an army the likes those Scots have never seen, and yea, even if death claims me in the effort, my bones will lead our charge into battle!"

And so it came to pass. King Edward I, often known as "Longshanks," barely out of his sickbed, passed away during the long trek north, leading his massive army recruited to decimate the "insolent forces" of Robert the Bruce.

Robert was now well on his way to freeing his native land from the English "hammer," but he had yet to confront the mighty English army heading north, determined to take away all vestiges of independence and freedom from English dominance.

"I cannot deal with this roughness of war," declared Edward's homosexual son, now King Edward II. "I am not as eager for revenge as my father." He returned to London, leaving Robert the Bruce to further consolidate his monarchy.

Robert now established a new government, the first Scottish government in eighteen years, and the fact that it was effective indicated the Scots were beginning to unite behind their king. All seemed to be going well for Robert, but soon once again the ogre of a powerful English army moving north intent on revenge raised its ugly head. Once again, Robert the Bruce knew he had to hold ground or perish.

"Where can we face and defeat the English this time?" inquired Robert's warlords as they met with their king near Stirling Castle. "They have such overwhelming numbers, and we are but five thousand men—mostly battle-hardened, but no match for the twenty thousand at Edward's disposal."

"We will win by strategy and guile," was Robert's plain reply.

Certainly strategy and guile became the order of the day on June 23, 1314, at a place called Bannockburn, in sight of Stirling Castle. Bannockburn itself lay only a few miles from the site of William Wallace's historic victory against another equally strong English army at the Battle of Stirling Bridge, some twenty years before.

"Sire, they look far too many for us to confront head-on," said Sir James as they stood looking at the massed English knights, archers, and infantry.

"Never fear," was Bruce's laconic reply. "We have ground advantage, we have local knowledge, we are not weighed down with armor, and we must surely have the good Lord with us. Who is that haughty sop of an English knight who rides so cockily to and fro, taunting and berating our stout-hearted troops?" he added. "I must be done with him."

The English knight was revealed to be one Sir Henry de Bohun. Robert rode forward and in full view of both armies, challenged Sir Henry to mortal combat. The result was never in doubt. Bruce, more lightly armored but with much greater mobility, first stuck down Sir Henry's horse from underneath the heavily armored knight and then with one mighty blow decapitated the arrogant de Bohun.

"Fall back, lads! Fall back beyond the swampy land!" shouted the Scottish commanders.

In pursuing the Scots, the English mounted cavalry fell into the line of pits the Scottish had prepared the previous day. The armored English horses were far too heavy for the soft ground; they sank and were immobilized. The Scots held the high ground, with the English too restricted to maneuver their horses.

"Fall upon them and spare neither soul nor life nor limb!" cried the Scottish officers.

Soon a momentous victory became reality for the five thousand loyal, battle-hardened veteran Scots. Many had been fighting the English for the two decades or so since William Wallace fought at Stirling Bridge. Many had been witness to Wallace's barbarous execution and Edward's devilling of the Wallace family, so this mighty victory came like manna from heaven, and no mercy was given to the hapless English leaders or their rank and file.

Edward II, Longshanks's son, barely escaped, leaving behind him all his baggage. Many of the retreating troops perished in the Bannock burn trying to run from the victorious Scots, and even more of Edward's foot soldiers drowned while fleeing through the treacherous bogs and putrid swampland surrounding them.

Bannockburn was the greatest victory the Scots ever won over the English. But despite their devastating loss, the English refused to accept the independence of Scotland, and raiding continued across the border for another fourteen years.

During this time, the Scottish church supported Bruce, but the church in Rome opposed him by supporting the English authority over Scotland as mandated by the late Edward Longshanks. This was no small matter for Bruce and his victorious men.

"We must send an appeal to the pope," declared Bruce to his gathered knights and nobles. "We will send the message contained in our Declaration of Arbroath, our declaration of independence and freedom from England. Surely he will see reason and renounce our nation's excommunication from the Church and recognize our country as blessed by the Lord Almighty."

The Scots not only told the pope what to do, but they also informed him their king ruled only by the will of the people, and only the people could remove him. The Declaration of Arbroath concluded: "Yet if he [the king] would give up what he has begun, and agree to make us or our kingdom subject to the king of England, we should exert ourselves to drive him out and make some other man who was well able to defend us, our king. For as long as but one hundred of us remain alive, never will we on any condition be brought under English rule. It is in truth, not for glory, not riches, not honors that we are fighting, but for freedom, for that alone which no honest man gives up but with life itself."

Despite the stirring sentiment and determination of the declaration, the pope waited four more years before acceding to the will of the Scots people and recognizing Bruce as king. By now the English no longer had the will or the desire to continue the war. With the exception of Durham Castle, Scottish raiders sacked all the northern English cities and towns. They even raided south to within fifty miles of London itself, causing great alarm and dismay.

Finally in 1328, a peace treaty acknowledging the independence of Scotland was signed, thus ending the twenty-six-year Scottish Wars of Independence, a final feather in the bonnet of the now battle-weary and sick King Robert.

"Come close, Sir James, my trusted friend, warlord, and defender of our faith," whispered Robert weakly, lying upon his deathbed covered with a gold-embroidered sheet. He sat up slowly and whispered almost inaudibly into Sir James Douglas's ear.

"I sinned most grievously against the good Lord when I killed John Comyn on the steps of Greyfriers Kirk. I desecrated his holy place, and I dearly seek atonement for what I have done. You, my dear Douglas—help me pass in peace, for I fear I will not see another morning. My time is nigh; my blood runs weakly through my shattered body, and I must make peace with my Lord before I leave this life. But Sir Douglas, if this I cannot do, maybe you will fulfill my wishes after death."

"Anything, my liege, anything for my brave and true leader," whispered Sir James as tears freely flowed from his near-closed eyes, dropping from his weathered cheeks onto the hand of King Robert, a hand he held close to his heaving chest.

"After I die, which I fear may be within the hour, you must take my heart from my chest, have it embalmed and placed in a silver casket, and take it with you on a crusade to the Holy Land. Once there, entomb it in the Church of the Holy Sepulcher in Jerusalem, and I, too, will then rest in peace," whispered the king.

"That will be my honor to do, my liege. I pledge my heart and soul to your wishes; your every desire is my command." And laying his head on his king's breast, Sir James listened to Robert's last breath as the life of his king finally ebbed away.

Robert Bruce had had no time to enjoy peace. The years of guerrilla warfare had taken their toll, and after only thirteen months of peace, Robert died at fifty-four years of age on June 7, 1329, leaving the throne to his five-year-old son, who became King David II

Chapter 3

A CHINESE CONNECTION

"Gentlemen, as bid by our dearly beloved and now lately departed King Robert, I have had his great and brave heart removed from his body. He now lies at peace in Dunfermline Abbey," said Sir James Douglas, casting his eye over some fifty knights, lords, and invited gentlemen gathered before him.

He turned and knelt before a small cloth-covered table on which lay a silver chain and a silver and enamel box. He bowed his bare head and crossed himself in silent prayer. All of the assembled company did likewise. After a few minutes, picking up the box, Sir James arose, turned to the now-standing company, and spoke again in an emotional and sometimes cracking voice.

"I have within this casket the heart of King Robert the Bruce, the bravest of all our late kings of Scots. I now place this casket, supported by this chain, around my neck. All present here today bear witness to my vow never to remove this chain and casket until I place them both upon the altar of the Church of the Holy Sepulcher in Jerusalem, or till they and I do part in death."

With great care and reverence, Sir James lifted the chain over his head, kissed the casket, and laid it gently against his heaving chest. Those closest to Sir James saw a few tears escape from his weary eyes, but soon he had regained control of his emotions and once again addressed the chosen few standing before him.

"It was Robert's dying wish that I take his heart to the Holy Land as part of a crusade to help free that land from the invading infidel. I have allowed for, and I am willing to give, five years of my life to carry out our dear departed Robert's last wish. I now stand before you asking, who of you will join me on this crusade leading to the placement of King Robert's heart upon the altar of the Church of the Holy Sepulcher in the city of Jerusalem?"

The assembled knights, lords, and gentlemen stood silent for some time, and then a hushed murmur arose as each man passed his thoughts to another. There was not much difference of opinion. All agreed that going to the Holy Land, as requested by the good Sir James, was a most honorable and praiseworthy action—but five years was a long time to leave home and family, especially during these turbulent times. Of course, Sir James knew it normally took several years to complete a successful crusade to the Holy Land, and many had turned back from their journey due to marauders such as the Saracens, who continually harassed and attacked them in the name of Allah. Sir James would not, under any circumstances, turn back. Only death would prevent him from completing his chosen task, and even then he would command in death his bones complete the journey.

A few anxious minutes passed before a tall, well-dressed, and well-spoken knight raised his right hand and addressed Sir James. "I am William de St. Clair of Roslin. I will be honored to travel by your side, Sir James. I and my retinue will be at your command for as long as it takes to accomplish our beloved Robert's dying wishes."

Another minute or so passed. One by one, knight and lord followed in like manner to William de St. Clair. Only a few slowly turned away with shoulders hunched, knowing within their hearts that they could not, with all good will, follow Sir James—not out of disloyalty, but almost all for reasons of family allegiance or matters of infirmity or immediate ill health. The die was cast; all who remained that day affirmed commitment to their Lord above and to King Robert the Bruce, their gallant and most patriotic leader those past twenty-six years.

And so, one bright spring day in the year 1330, Sir James Douglas departed the Scottish border town of Berwick-upon-Tweed for the port of Sluys on the Dutch coast to begin his journey to the Holy Land. Traveling with him were one knight bannerette, seven ordinary knights, twenty-six esquires, and a retinue in proportion. Included in the group were Sir Simon Lochart of Lee, Sir William de Keith, Sir William de St. Clair of Roslin, Sir Alan Cathcart, the brothers of Sir Robert Logan of Restalrig, and Sir Walter Logan.

They remained twelve days at Sluys, allowing knights from all over Europe to join the party. King Edward III of England had provided a safe conduct for the knights and a letter of recommendation to King Alfonso of Spain. They arrived in Seville at the end of July. The whole company was well received by the Spaniards and others already gathered there to join a crusade organized by King Alfonso XI of Castile against the Muslims of the kingdom of Granada. Sir James and his entourage were received by Alfonso with great distinction upon arriving by sea at Seville.

"Sir James, we have three monks from Scone Abbey requesting to join us, along with their friend—a tall, broad-shouldered Mongolian warrior who has traveled to Europe with his Christian brothers and now fallen on hard times," said Sir Walter Logan, ushering in the monks and the new warrior.

"Who sent you to join us?" inquired Sir James of the monks who now lay prone before him.

The monks stood up, facing Sir James, and the tallest replied.

"The abbot of Scone himself directed us to find you, accompany you, and pray for you each day and night. He has also blessed the heart you carry, a heart he was unable to bless at Robert the Bruce's coronation—a coronation without the Bruce sitting upon the Stone of Destiny."

"I have known your abbot well these past thirty years, and if that be his desire, you are all welcome to carry out his wishes. But tell me about this Mongolian warrior standing at your side."

"His name is Wu Zeng," replied one of the monks, "and he claims to be the son of Guyuk, a descendent of the great Genghis Khan."

"He is one of the few Christian Chinese who visited the courts of Europe some years ago," added a second monk. "However, as a young man he was kidnapped by wandering gypsies in southern France and only recently escaped and joined us just after we left Sluys. He now seeks your indulgence and requests safe passage from King Alfonso to return to his native land. Once there, he hopes to reclaim his inheritance and also claim his rightful title, emperor of the present Yang Dynasty, a title now held illegally by his younger brother."

Sir James conferred a few minutes with his second-in-command, Sir William de Keith, and then, turning to the four standing in front of him, he said, "Your wishes are granted, but other than fighting in self-defense if attacked, you holy men should only perform your Christian duties and pray for us both day and night. You, Wu Zeng, may also stay until the way is clear for your return to China. You need to conserve your energies for the long journey you have ahead after we reach the Holy Land. I request that you take no part in any hostilities other than to protect your own life."

Having joined King Alfonso's Crusade, Sir James and his Scottish contingent were also duty-bound to fight for King Alfonso during the Spanish king's efforts to overcome the Saracen army now blocking their way to the Holy Land.

At Teba on August 25, 1330, a great and memorable battle commenced. Sir James and his company soon came into view of the Saracens near the Castillo de la Estrella at Teba, on the frontiers of Andalucía. The Castilian trumpets sounded the Spanish attack, and Sir James led his troops forward, thinking a general advance order had been given. However, this turned out to be a false assumption, as the opposing Moorish king had ordered a body of three thousand cavalry to make a feigned attack on the Spaniards while the great body of his army took a circling route to fall upon the rear of Alfonso's camp. Alfonso, however, having received intelligence, kept the main force of his army in the rear, while resisting the assault made on the front division of his army.

With the battle brought to a successful conclusion on one quarter of the field, Sir James and his companions who fought in the vanguard were equally successful in their initial attack. The Moors, not long able to withstand the furious onslaught, fled. Unacquainted with their mode of warfare, Sir James followed them until he found himself almost deserted by his followers. He turned his horse with the intention of re-joining the main body. Just then, however, he observed a knight of his own company, surrounded by a body of Moors who had suddenly rallied. With the few knights who attended him, Sir James turned hastily to attempt rescue. He soon found himself hard pressed by overwhelming numbers of Moorish forces who thronged upon and around him.

Taking from his neck the chain and silver casket that contained the heart of the Bruce, he stood in the saddle and leading one last furious and gallant attack, he cast the chain and casket ahead of him into the enemy ranks, and shouted loud so all could hear, "Now pass thou onward before us, as thou were often wont to do. I will forever follow thee, Braveheart, even unto certain death!"

Sir James Douglas and almost all the men who fought by his side were slain during this last legendary assault, including Sir

William de St. Clair of Roslin and Sir Robert Logan. When all was over, the mutilated body of Sir James was found lying atop the casket containing Bruce's heart. He had indeed followed his Braveheart unto death, along with his other followers who also lay dead surrounding him.

The Moors, seeing that their own overwhelming numbers would surely win the day, were content to surround and capture those of the Scottish company who remained alive and tended to the wounded, ensuring that a few others also survived.

A few days later, the Moorish king stood before the gathered band of gallant survivors, the three monks, and Wu Zeng, and addressed them thus: "Never have I seen such a ferocious assault by so few upon so many. We are proud to have been your honored foes this day. I grant you all free passage to return home, taking with you the body of your fallen leader and the silver casket he wore. Good fortune and safe journey, most gallant and worthy foes."

The survivors of the Scottish contingent were well looked after by their Spanish friends. They were given medical attention, food, drink, and shelter, and within a few weeks were ready to return to Scotland, taking with them the body of Sir James Douglas and the casket containing Bruce's heart. They were led by Sir William de Keith and Sir Simon Lockhart, the only surviving knights, but the three monks from Scone Abbey and Wu Zeng elected not to return to Scotland but to continue on to the Holy Land. Before the main party left, there was a meeting between Sir William de Keith, the monks, and Wu Zeng. Only minutes remained before the two parties were to divide and start upon their separate journeys. The group led by Sir William was to travel north to Scotland by sea; the other, overland to Jerusalem.

"Sir William," one of the monks began, "we have a special talisman given us by the abbot of Scone, which we must now give into your care and protection. This small casket was intended for Sir James Douglas, but we now desire you take it back with you to Scotland."

Sir William took the casket—similar in size and shape to the one containing King Robert the Bruce's heart—and inquired as to its purpose.

"Within this casket lies the answer to the location of our Coronation Stone, the genuine Stone of Destiny, hidden before King Edward's armies arrived to take it to England," replied the senior monk. "Guard it with your life. Upon returning to Robert Bruce's last resting place, leave it where no man will find it until the 'fist of Bruce' rises again to indicate another King of Scots will rule a newborn kingdom. This will be a kingdom yearned for and voted for by that country's longsuffering people but will not become reality for many years, even centuries."

Sir William seemed taken aback at this new turn of affairs—this supreme responsibility to those who had fallen beside him a few weeks ago. He looked skyward a few moments and then sank to one knee, with both hands crossed in prayer, and replied, "This request I swear to do. I will perform everything within my power to preserve and defend this most precious of objects. I will never fail your trust in me and will treasure the honor you have given me to safeguard the relics of our nation."

He kissed the sealed silver casket three times and then placed it carefully in one of his saddlebags.

"Our trust and faith are in you, Sir William," said the third monk. "We cannot ask for more; we know you will not fail us."

All three monks and Wu Zeng bowed in reverence to Sir William. They turned eastward and within a few minutes started on their way to the Holy Land.

It took the remaining Scots, under the leadership of Sir William de Keith and Sir Simon Lockhart, two months to journey back to Scotland. They were met by the Earl of Moray, acting as regent for young King David II, who had already been advised of the tragic happenings at the Battle of Teba. There were no great celebrations, just a somber welcome and condolences for the heartbreaking family losses.

A week or so after arriving back in Scotland, the remains of Sir James Douglas were deposited in his family's vaults at St. Bride's Chapel in south Lanarkshire. The heart of Bruce, contained in the casket worn by Douglas, was solemnly interred by Moray under the high altar of Melrose Abbey. The casket would remain untouched for the next seven hundred years.

The three monks and Wu Zeng were able to speak to one another in French, but more often they conversed in Latin. Wu Zeng had told the monks the installation of a new emperor in the Yang Dynasty required the emperor to sit upon a stone chair, similar to the ritual carried out at Scone Abbey for the coronation of Scottish kings. The stone used among his people was believed to have been hewn from the very same site as the Stone of Destiny—also known as "Jacob's Pillow." Wu Zeng needed to find the original site to allow him to chisel off a small part of the stone and then return to China with the chiseled stone in his possession. None but the rightful heirs to the title of emperor knew the location where the Emperor Stone had been hewn. Having this knowledge and a piece of stone similar in color and density to the Emperor Stone would help Wu Zeng substantiate his claim to power.

Just before entering the Holy Land, the monks and Wu Zeng encountered some priests of the Levite cult. These Levites welcomed them and shared their own shelter and food for a number of days. When asked the whereabouts of Jacob's Pillow, one of the Levites replied, "You must go to Bethel, the House of God, and look for the ladder stretching between heaven and earth. There you will find the greater part of the stone your people call the *Lia Fail*. This stone, having been anointed with holy oil, has been split into at least two parts, and those parts carried great distances both north and east in the name of Israel, our forefather Jacob's adopted name. Jacob dreamed of this ladder rising from the stone up to heaven, thronged with angels."

"You must direct us to this place called Bethel," requested Wu Zeng. "There I must recover part of the original stone, thus proving my identity and confirming my rightful status of emperor, my inherited destiny."

"Then you must travel to the Northern Kingdom of Israel, about ten miles north of Jerusalem, and ask for the ancient city of Luz—a Canaanite name—and there inquire further," replied one of the elder priests.

The three monks and Wu Zeng traveled north for seven days before entering the ancient city now called Babel. Some friendly priests soon guided the four travelers toward the greater part of the original *Lia Fail*, a stone that seemed to consist of white marble.

"Wu Zeng, you have no need to look further," said the elder monk. "When the abbot of Scone hid the original Stone of Destiny from King Edward's armies, he chiseled off part of the stone, and that very part I now have with me. The wise abbot did this to ensure positive identification of the original stone, in both color and material, by comparison with the stone used during the coronation of your Yang Dynasty emperors. Some twenty years before the arrival of King Edward's men, as a young monk, this same abbot had traveled here, as you have done. He was charged with fitting another part of the Stone of Destiny with the original Jacob's Pillow. This he did, thus proving the authenticity of the Stone of Destiny as also part of this marble block we see before us now."

After a short pause, the monk continued. "The abbot of Scone to whom I have just referred regrettably died, taking the secret hiding place of the Stone of Destiny with him to his Maker. I am the abbot-elect, and it is my sworn task to prove that another stone exists, hewn from the same pillar at about the same time. If this is true, I will have found at least part of the truth, and a positive clue to enhance our search for the Stone of Destiny's hiding place."

The monk turned a piercing glance on the Mongol warrior. "You too, Wu Zeng, must take a part of this pillar from which your emperors' coronation stone was hewn, and compare that fragment with your Emperor's Stone, so proving your authentic claim to lead the Yang Dynasty."

Taking the monk's advice, Wu Zeng chiseled a small part of the pillar he thought most likely to fit in color and composition with the Emperor's Stone and placed it safely within his traveling bag.

The abbot-elect then continued. "Wu Zeng, I have here another small silver casket, similar to the one carried to Scotland by Sir William de Keith with the body of Sir James Douglas. Take it with you, along with your fragment of the *Lia Fail*—and as we charged Sir Henry, guard it with your life. Deposit the casket safely beneath your own Emperor Stone when you have regained your rightful position. Within this casket lie three tokens and a stone chip. The tokens will eventually be given to three native Scots of unblemished birthright, all directly descended from our late King Robert. That time may be centuries in the future, but when Bruce's clenched fist rises again, you or your successor will be given a sign to take actions ensuring a Scottish king will once again rule over a Scottish kingdom and a free nation."

A few days passed, during which time the monks and Wu Zeng prepared themselves for their respective long journeys. The monks set off to Scotland first. They took a sea passage to the south of France and then traveled overland once again to Sluys, and thence to Berwick, from where they had set sail two years before. Wu Zeng prepared to return to his native land via the Silk Road made known by Marco Polo many years before, the same road Wu Zeng had traveled westward more than two decades earlier before his captive years.

Once warm and sincere farewells were made, and after wishing each other safe and successful journeys, the four travelers parted, never to meet again.

Chapter 4

THE BRUCE ASSERTION

April 2008

Angus Gillespie, PhD, one-time dean of the department of archaeology at Edinburgh University, gave off the aura of being an absent-minded professor. However, in reality, he was not anything even approaching that description. He had been recognized worldwide by many in academia, particularly in the area of medieval archaeology, as the very best in Europe. Angus had contracted a serious, body-ravaging disease (never fully diagnosed) during his extensive travels throughout the Middle East while concentrating on his research and excavations within the Holy Land. Now, although still fully alert, he had acquired a distinct stoop and ungainly stride, which had become more pronounced during his retirement years. However, being physically handicapped did not impair his active mind and meticulous memory. Angus still worked part-time from his old office, a facility granted him for life by his college, and immersed himself in the many ongoing projects he had been involved with during his last few years' tenure at the university.

Being of Scottish birth, Angus had consistently championed the cause of those scholars convinced the Stone of Destiny was very much a reality, not a figment of nationalistic imagination. He certainly did not go along with the premise that the stone now lying in Edinburgh castle was the genuine stone upon which all ancient kings of Scotland sat during their coronation ceremonies. His meticulous research had convinced him and his close colleagues the original stone had been part of the marble block situated in Babel. They believed it was only a matter of time before the forces of Christendom would reveal the stone's current resting place. This belief was validated by newfound evidence that verified the disclosure of some monks two centuries ago. These disclosures, when acted on by reliable archaeologists, had revealed the whereabouts of a similar stone chiseled from the Lia Fail about the same time. That stone had been spirited away to Mongolia and used as a coronation chair for the Yang Dynasty emperors during the many years that dynasty had been in power.

Angus had never married. He had many relationships as a younger man, but since being struck down with polio some forty-five years before, there had really only been one woman in his life: Elizabeth Walker. Elizabeth had worked under Angus at the Edinburgh facility; however, the rhetorical meaning of "under" had over the years became a physical meaning, and Elizabeth and Angus shared a pleasant eighteenth-century cottage located on the Elgin Estates. These estates were not far from his workplace in Edinburgh and only ten minutes' drive from Dunfermline Abbey, where much of his private archaeological work had been concentrated.

Over the years, Angus had become increasingly convinced a connection existed between the death and internment of King Robert the Bruce and the whereabouts of the original stone. He certainly believed a connection existed between the Scottish Stone and the Chinese Stone, both having been used for similar coronation purposes and both having been supposedly hewn from the same slab of marble in the Holy Land. Angus was obviously not present when Bruce's body was exhumed in 1818. But that exhumation confirmed to an excited Scottish public that indeed Bruce's ribs had been sawn through, indicating his heart had undeniably been taken from his body, thus proving that legend true. Angus always argued, "If this part of the legend was true, why not the rest?"

The excavation of Melrose Abbey in 1921 went a long way toward justifying the hopes and predictions of many Scottish historians and archaeologists. In the summer of 1921, during excavations beneath the Chapter House at Melrose Abbey, a conical leaden casket was discovered. It measured ten inches high and four inches in diameter at the base, but it tapered toward the top. It was pitted but otherwise in good condition. After a cursory examination by the local workmen and some local, less-than-qualified archaeological staff, it was suitably annotated and reburied that same year in about the same place the casket was found.

In the summer of 1996, excavations of the Chapter House floor of Melrose Abbey were carried out by Historic Scotland archaeological staff. On Monday, September 3, the team from Historic Scotland investigated a silver and enamel container said to contain King Robert the Bruce's heart. This container had been removed from beneath the Chapter House floor the previous week.

Under laboratory conditions, a small hole was drilled into the casket and the interior investigated by fiber-optic cable. This casket was then carefully opened. Inside was another small conical lead casket and a copper plaque inscribed as follows:

THE ENCLOSED LEADEN CASKET CONTAINING A HEART WAS FOUND BENEATH THIS

CHAPTER HOUSE FLOOR, MARCH 1921, BY HIS MAJESTY'S OFFICE OF WORKS

The investigating team from Historic Scotland said, "Although it is not possible to absolutely prove that it is Bruce's heart, it is reasonable to assume so. There are no records of anyone else's heart being buried at Melrose."

On June 22, 1998, the casket was reburied at Melrose Abbey two days before the anniversary of Bruce's victory at Bannockburn in 1314. A plaque was laid above the casket's burial place, and on it was engraved the words:

A NOBLE HEART MAY HAVE NO EASE, GIF FREEDOM FAILYE.

Translated, this reads: "A noble heart cannot be at peace if freedom is lacking."

Angus and Elizabeth and all of the team were greatly encouraged by the find. They felt the answer to locating the original stone was most likely in yet another casket. This second casket was allegedly brought back by Sir William de Keith after the battle of Teba in 1330 at the same time as the casket containing Bruce's heart.

Sir William appeared to have been successful in hiding the casket containing the answer to the whereabouts of the genuine Stone of Destiny. Many had tried to solve the mystery without any success, but Angus genuinely believed he, with the help of the lovely and devoted Elizabeth, would be the one to succeed where so many before had failed. He felt he alone had the determination, insight, and archaeological know-how that others were lacking, and most importantly, he felt finding the stone was his fate from birth.

"Elizabeth, we must travel to China and see the Emperor Stone, and we must seek out all knowledge retained by the Buddhist monks who have kept the secret of their Coronation Stone for so long," said Angus.

Angus continued, "We may be able to carry out the necessary covert investigations while completing my earlier Chinese Dynasty archaeological studies."

Elizabeth countered, "Yes, Angus, and who exactly do you expect to be your obedient servant this time? I am getting too old for journeys of this length. The Holy Land trips were fine, but to go to China is quite different," she responded.

"We have been together far too many years to part over this trip. Would you rather I go by myself and possibly die alone—so far away from you?" replied Angus.

Elizabeth thought long and hard over the next few days. She had loved Angus for over thirty years had been with him through thick and thin. But she knew time was running out rather quickly for them both.

She finally gave him an answer. "Angus, I will not let you run out on me at this stage in our lives, so I will come this last time, but very much against my better judgment. I only hope your judgment will result in honor for us both."

Elizabeth committed herself to one last journey, which she believed to be yet another lost cause.

During his tenure at Edinburgh University, Angus had shown great curiosity regarding the mysterious history of the medieval Rosslyn Chapel (of *The Da Vinci Code* fame). That chapel, built over seven hundred years ago, lay seven miles to the southwest of the city. Angus had made many trips there studying the mysterious carvings and signs. He continuously tried to make some sense of the carvings that clearly referred to Crusader knights, kings, the Catholic Church, and the influences of Freemasonry and the Knights Templar. All this he did with little or no real success. However, Angus had increasingly come to believe the answer to the Stone of Destiny mystery lay buried within the unopened vaults beneath the chapel floor.

Angus was at hand when Dr. Lun Yin, a renowned archaeology professor, visited the chapel. Angus and Dr. Yin had often met before in the Middle East. Dr. Yin was a prominent Buddhist. He had visited many cathedrals and ancient chapels worldwide, but he had never before come across such an intriguing place as Rosslyn which exuded such "fengshui." His remarks were echoed by most of the other experts accompanying him from Mongolia, China, Korea, and other Far East countries. Angus's interest leapt immediately upon hearing Dr. Yin's subdued remarks of, "intriguing, intriguing, what an exceptional coincidence" when he viewed the supposed death mask of King Robert the Bruce that hung in the chapel. Angus immediately determined to question Dr. Yin further at a reception to be held later that evening in the old Scottish Parliament Hall.

"Doctor Yin, can you tell me about the thoughts you had when viewing the death mask of King Robert the Bruce earlier today?" inquired Angus during an opportune moment at the evening reception for the visiting archaeologists.

Dr. Yin seemed mildly surprised at Angus's question, but he was familiar with Angus and his reputation and consequently asked Angus to step aside a few minutes, allowing them to speak more openly.

"When I was a young man, I became very interested in researching the Yang Dynasty. During my research, I learned of our third emperor, Wu Zeng, and his well-documented travels to the Middle East during the early fourteenth century. There he was befriended by some monks from Scotland. He eventually returned to Mongolia to claim his rightful place as emperor, bringing with him a talisman in the form of a small silver casket. Legend says within this casket lay secret instruction regarding the succession of kings of Scotland and when that succession would arise again."

"Where is that casket now, and where was it found?" asked Angus.

"With the coming of communism to my country, I believe the casket and accompanying instructions were spirited away to Lantau Island, in Hong Kong. There the casket was kept by Buddhist monks, and I believe it remains there to this day," replied Dr. Yin.

"And where was the casket found and when?" inquired Angus.

"The date I do not know, but certainly many years after Emperor Zeng's passing, and then only when the emperor's burial place was excavated for relocation purposes. The casket was found under the emperor's embalmed body in as good a condition as the day it was brought from the Holy Land," replied Dr. Yin.

"But why did you show such emotion when you saw the death mask of Robert the Bruce?" pressed Angus, now very intrigued.

"A parchment written in an ancient Latin based language was found inside the casket, along with three unusual coins or metal tokens. The parchment referred to Robert the Bruce and his hands, and I remember the translation being very odd and not making any sense," continued Dr. Yin.

"Can you remember what the translation said exactly?" asked a slightly impatient Angus.

"It said something like, 'Scots will only rule their homeland after the clenched fist of Bruce rises once again.'"

Angus was dumbstruck. He found it hard to believe the answer could now be within his grasp and only a few miles away from home.

After listening to Dr. Yin's explanation, Angus's interest soared to new heights. He knew Wu Zeng had been in touch with the monks of Scone seven hundred years ago, and he instinctively knew the answer to the Stone of Destiny's whereabouts probably lay within Dunfermline Abbey. This abbey stood only a few miles from his residence, a place where he had concentrated much of his research in earlier years.

"There will be no need for a journey to China," said Angus to Elizabeth.

"But I think a trip to talk with the abbot or a senior Buddhist monk attached to Po Lin Monastery on Lantau Island, a few miles offshore from Hong Kong, would be invaluable," he continued.

"Hong Kong sounds wonderful to me," replied Elizabeth, remembering the good shopping she experienced when visiting there a few years ago.

Landing at the new international airport named Chek-Lap-Kok on Lantau Island was quite different from landing at the old airport of Kai Tak. Approaches from either direction into Kai Tak were singularly hazardous. Landing on either end of the runway, depending on wind direction, required a steep descent down to the runway over densely populated high-rise buildings. Approaches into the new airport, not far from the Po Lin Monastery, were mostly over open sea. The new runway was long enough for even the largest most heavily loaded aircraft to take off and land safely, well within the aircraft's safety margins.

Angus and Elizabeth very much enjoyed their times in Hong Kong over the years. During four visits, they also traveled over the border into mainland China, but visits to the mainland then had been much more difficult regarding the issue of visas. Now, after the British authorities had handed back the colony to China in 1998, visas were processed and issued without undue delay, but the cost of visas had risen considerably. Angus decided there was really no need to get visas for travel into mainland China. He could do everything he wanted in Hong Kong, and anyway, the visa costs were prohibitive.

"Elizabeth, this will probably be our last trip to Hong Kong. Let's do all the things we had hoped to do before and failed to accomplish, and let's hope I will find another piece in the puzzle of the Stone of Destiny mystery," said Angus just before their British Airways Jumbo Jet touched down.

"Angus, how nice this is going to be. I am sure you will find what you have sought so passionately these many years," replied Elizabeth, now almost overcome with the excitement of once again roaming the streets and markets of her most favorite of cities.

Once clearing immigration and customs, the trip into Kowloon using the MTR (Mass Transport Railway) was quick and spectacular. The spotless electric train passed over bustling waterways, above and through immense bridge flyovers, and close to the massive container ship terminal of Tsuen Wan. Soon the high-rise buildings of Western Kowloon were left behind and their set-down station of Tsim Sha Tsui was upon them after only twenty minutes' travel from the airport. Angus had spared no expense, and soon he and Elizabeth were checking into the Intercontinental Hotel, renowned for spectacular views both day and night over Hong Kong's inner harbor.

"Angus, how wonderful, you remembered my dream to stay here, even for one night! Thank you, thank you, my dear," replied Elizabeth with affection.

Angus gave a smile of self-contentment he usually reserved for making his loved one happy and radiant.

After Angus had sent a request for an audience with the abbot of Po Lin Monastery, he and Elizabeth spent a few special days wandering the streets and markets of Hong Kong Island and Kowloon. They revisited many of their haunts of years past, such as the "forbidden city" in Kowloon (now opened up to allow visitors to enter since the return of Hong Kong to China in 1998), Cat Street on Hong Kong Island, and Stanley Market, where both Angus and Elizabeth were recognized by some of the shopkeepers. Angus loved Cantonese food. He considered none finer than the dishes served on the famous Jumbo Floating Restaurant anchored in Aberdeen Bay near the south side of Hong Kong Island. Here they spent two lovely evenings together savoring the unique taste of genuine Cantonese cooking.

Elizabeth insisted on traveling to the top of the Peak on Hong Kong Island one last time riding the old funicular tramway to get there. Once arrived at the upper tramway station, sixteen hundred feet above the harbor, she and Angus took one last walk round the Peak using Lugard Road. This "road" was really only a few feet wide and would be more correctly described as a footpath. The visibility and weather were excellent, and they were able to have one last memorable all-round view of Hong Kong as they completed their circular walk back to the tram station.

On the evening of the fourth day, Angus received word that the abbot would be happy to meet with him anytime during the following day between the times of afternoon prayer and meditation. Angus and he should meet only by themselves. Elizabeth, although disappointed at not being able to meet the abbot, was still happy to accompany Angus and see part of the monastery and also view and climb the new 150-foot Buddha that had been erected almost a year after their last visit.

Angus and Elizabeth set out well before noon for Lantau Island. After a forty-five-minute ferry ride, they landed at Silver Mine Bay's arrival pier, and after wandering through the many clothing and electrical goods stalls, they had a small Cantonese lunch consisting of fresh seafood and dim sum. Soon they boarded a blue double-decker bus that took them up five winding miles to the esplanade in front of the Po Lin Monastery. The trip proved very interesting for them both. They passed through many small villages, looked out over terraced fields growing all sorts of vegetables, and stopped a few times to allow farmers to herd their cows and pigs across the road from field to field. The bus ride took almost one hour. Many local people were gathered around small temples beside the main entrance. There, many Buddhist pilgrims lit joss sticks and offered prayers to their ancestors, and the sweet smell of smoke hung heavily in the air. Angus and Elizabeth continued further into the monastery through a series of doors and arches until they came to the monks' living quarters. It was here Angus was to meet the abbot, and a large sign in various languages proclaimed, "No Visitors Beyond This Point." Angus asked Elizabeth to wait by the door but added she could look at other parts of the inner monastery grounds provided she returned to the door every half hour. Angus said he would meet her there without having to look for her all over the people-filled grounds.

Angus pressed the large brass doorbell, and within a few seconds the door was opened by a young monk dressed in the black attire of a novice.

"Doctor Angus, please come in and follow me," said the monk in broken English. "The abbot will meet with you in a few minutes. Please wait here." With those words, he ushered Angus into a small reception room.

The room was almost completely round and had a small, circular, heavily decorated rug on the stone floor lying under a round teak table situated in the center of the room. The walls were covered with what Angus took to be ancient tapestries from central China. Two wooden chairs beside the round table completed the austere furnishings, and Angus was directed to one of them to await the abbot's arrival. Within a few minutes, the sound of a muted gong announced the abbot's arrival into the room. He was clothed in a loose-fitting saffron-colored robe. He was of medium height and looked a little overweight, but had a kind-looking oval-shaped face. He sat down upon one of the chairs.

"I am very pleased to meet you. My name is Au Ling San. What can I do for you, my most distinguished of visitors?" began the abbot, speaking in low tones but surprisingly with no pronounced accent.

"Mister Au, I recently talked with a Doctor Yin with whom I believe you are familiar," started Angus. The abbot nodded his head. "The good doctor and I discussed the whereabouts of a small silver casket removed from mainland China after the communists took over in 1948. This casket he believed was here at Po Lin under your care and protection," explained Angus. Then he continued, "I would be very honored and deeply indebted to you and your monastery if you could give me permission to examine that casket for archaeological and historical reasons. It may help solve a great mystery surrounding the coronation of ancient kings of Scotland. I and my fellow countrymen and government would be forever grateful if you grant me this privilege."

"We do have the casket you speak of, and yes, you may inspect it. Regrettably, only a few years ago, the casket was examined and all contents removed by unknown persons during the dead of night," replied the abbot with some genuine regret in his voice.

"Was the casket not well protected?" asked Angus

"Yes, it was protected by our peacocks. Peacocks are fine guards; they screech and call when anyone they do not know approaches where we keep the casket together with other valuables removed with the casket from mainland China in 1948. Only the casket seemed to be tampered with after the break-in," continued the abbot.

"So how were the intruders able to get near without the peacocks raising the alarm?" questioned Angus.

"Oh, they were very shrewd and cunning," continued the abbot. "They left a small sack of alcohol-soaked grain for the peacocks to feed on. After the peacocks had eaten enough grain, the alcohol took effect and the peacocks did not raise any alarm. Very clever, really, and no obvious harm befell the birds," explained the abbot.

Angus stood dumbfounded. Was he to be foiled and disappointed yet again?

"I would still like to examine the casket," said Angus.

"You surely may," replied the abbot and instructed the waiting novice to bring the casket to him at once.

Angus related most of the story about the Stone of Destiny, and the abbot confirmed the legend concerning the third emperor of the Yang Dynasty and the dynasty's association with a similar stone. Soon the novice returned, carrying a small silver casket lying upon a velvet cushion.

Angus gazed in awe. He had waited many years for this opportunity, and now everything could depend on what lay before him.

"Can I open the lid?" inquired Angus.

"Yes, please do, it is quite loose," replied the abbot.

Angus could see immediately there was nothing inside, but there definitely had been. Three slot-like indentations clearly showed where some coin-like objects had been fitted.

"Were there three coins here when you viewed the contents years ago?" asked Angus.

"Yes, indeed there were," replied the abbot. "Those three coins are all that appear to have been stolen; I cannot think why."

"I think I know the answer to your question, but it will be a long time in proving. Can I take some photographs to show my colleagues in Scotland?" asked Angus.

"Yes, of course, but you must promise the photographs will not be published and will only be used to further your research," warned the abbot.

"I give you my word," said Angus as he took several pictures with his digital camera.

Angus, after expressing his most sincere gratitude to the abbot, said his farewells. After leaving the interview, he met with Elizabeth as planned, and both started back to their hotel. Their journey this time was by an equally tortuous route down the north side of the island toward the international airport. Once at the airport, it was an easy matter to board one of the electric mass transport trains to a station near their hotel.

All through the return journey, Angus remained silent. He seemed to be in some sort of trance. Elizabeth knew better than to try even the shortest of conversations. However, things changed dramatically once they were back in their hotel room. At last Angus felt free. He almost exploded with the release of all the excitement he had contained inside himself since meeting with the abbot.

"Elizabeth, I believe I now know where the answer lies," he blurted out with such enthusiasm and speed Elizabeth could hardly understand his words.

"What do you think you know? We have had false starts and disappointments so many times before, I can barely remember them all," she countered.

"Elizabeth, the answer is with the Bruce in Dunfermline Abbey. I feel my heart, soul, and body, and even my very bones are guiding me in that direction."

"But was it not Melrose Abbey, one hundred miles south of Dunfermline, where his heart was found! Were you not there at the last internment of the silver casket when you were working with Historic Scotland? Why now Dunfermline Abbey?" she asked.

"Since talking with Doctor Yin and viewing the casket at Po Lin monastery, a great deal has changed within my mind. Have faith in me, and much will be revealed," concluded Angus with a wry smile on his ageing face.

Nothing more of the happenings at Po Lin passed the lips of either Angus or Elizabeth during their last two days in Hong Kong. Both were maybe too deep in thought about each other's perception of events, Angus optimistic in the extreme, Elizabeth much less so. However, she thought to herself there may be new reason to hope.

After almost twenty-four hours of traveling, both were exhausted on arrival at their cottage and slept for over twelve hours.

Chapter 5

A TOMB'S SECRET

Although Angus no longer worked for Historic Scotland, he still retained an honorary directorship, and his input and counsel were much sought after. He had carried out some archival work and given a few lectures on modern archaeology. His honorary work and free lectures were much appreciated and respected by both the university and Historic Scotland. Both organizations had called upon him frequently to lecture in recent months when staff had been indisposed or engaged carrying out university-sponsored expeditions overseas.

Angus felt both organizations owed him some favors in view of all the work he had volunteered, especially work concerning the life and times of King Robert the Bruce. But it was his investigative efforts regarding the Stone of Destiny on which he now felt he should focus all his efforts. For the past twenty-five years or so, he had been regarded as the foremost expert on all subjects concerning the Stone of Destiny. He felt it was now time for him to ask a great favor: permission to re-investigate the tomb of King Robert the Bruce.

"Elizabeth, I need to have a meeting with the director of Historic Scotland to convince him of my new theory and intentions," stated Angus during breakfast a few days after their return from Hong Kong.

"Well, Angus, this seems to be yet another departure from standard protocol," commented Elizabeth, hardly looking up from the table. "Do tell me what these new intentions entail," quizzed Elizabeth.

"I am convinced another casket having similar contents to the one I looked at in the monastery lies within or close to the tomb of King Robert in Dunfermline Abbey," explained Angus.

Angus felt relieved at having confided his thoughts and hopes to Elizabeth, whom he knew to be most skeptical. However, he was still confident in his all-consuming theory and continued.

"There were drawings made of the coffin's contents, the positioning of the embalmed body and limbs, and the exact location of some Masonic regalia believed to belong to the king. Remember, King Robert was reputed to have been the founder of the Scottish Masonic Order shortly after the Battle of Bannockburn,"

Elizabeth listened more intently as Angus continued; things were beginning to make some sense.

"I have copies of those original drawings, now part of the Old Library of Scotland's ancient document collection, and I need to compare them with what today lies within the coffin. Although there has been some movement of the coffin since 1818 for re-interment, the coffin has supposedly not been reopened. I need to confirm this."

"Angus, can I advise you to leave well enough alone? Remember the fate of those in the mid-1930s who insisted on opening the Tomb of Tutankhamen? They all died shortly after under mysterious circumstances," Elizabeth warned. Then she added, "Although I would be worried for your safety if you opened the tomb, I must admit in this case there is no known curse on Bruce's tomb, whereas there was a curse upon those opening Tutankhamen's tomb."

"My dear, all those men were in midlife with much to live for. I am at the end of my life and would willingly die after I successfully found the Stone of Destiny, but of course, only after you!" Angus countered.

"Well, Angus, after all these years together, that observation is a great comfort to me!" replied Elizabeth, visibly shaken at Angus's heartless vision of their future together.

"Sorry, dear," replied Angus. "What I really meant alluded to those archaeologists doing much against, and in spite of, local disapproval. There had been a history of those tombs being ransacked, and the local people had sworn revenge. I believe there was no curse and those deaths were associated with some form of reprisal. Dunfermline's inhabitants and all Scottish people would welcome another exhumation if doing so resulted in solving the mystery concerning the location of the original, genuine Stone of Destiny. I am sure no harm would befall me or anyone assisting us."

Elizabeth seemed more at ease upon hearing Angus's thoughts.

The wheels of government departments tend to turn slowly, especially for someone with little or no patience. After petitioning every government department having anything to do with archaeological digs, including exhumation, and having received at best a lukewarm interest, he turned to a more direct, albeit somewhat devious, approach.

Over the years, Angus had produced numerous papers and press releases and edited many articles published by government organizations without acknowledgment. For some time now, much of his work had been plagiarized and articles had been reproduced without his permission. In many cases, he only knew about this illegal practice when he recognized some of his work in publications where his writings had been reproduced without his knowledge.

"I will bring pressure to bear upon the directors of all the historical organizations, government departments, and other publishers of my unauthorized work. They will surely sanction my request to complete a further exhumation of King Robert the Bruce's tomb. I know from experience many would not risk being exposed as plagiarists if my request was not looked upon favorably," said Angus to Elizabeth and some of his closest staff late one Friday afternoon.

A few weeks later, Angus received the permission he dearly sought, and secret arrangements were made for the exhumation of King Robert the Bruce whenever Angus thought the time suitable. Angus lost little time, and soon all was prepared.

Angus was well aware of the long and important history surrounding Dunfermline Abbey, so he proceeded with due care and reverence.

When Queen Margaret married Malcolm III in the year 1070, Dunfermline was already a place of royal residence. Margaret founded a Benedictine priory there, and her third son, King David I, raised it to abbey status in 1128. The abbey is the chosen burial place of eight kings, four queens, five princes, and two princesses. In addition, William Wallace's mother, Margaret, is buried there, and in the sixteenth century the abbey guest house was converted into a royal palace.

Over the centuries, the exact location of Robert the Bruce's grave became obscure. In 1818, when the ground was being cleared in preparation for the building of a new abbey church, workmen came across a vault that was found to be built of polished masonry. Within the vault was an oak coffin covered with two sheets of lead, and inside the coffin laid a shroud of gold cloth. After a short examination, the tomb was closed again until the following year when an official inspection was made; it was then the drawings were completed.

Angus knew he did not have an easy job on his hands; however, this time exhumation would be easier than when previously carried out. When Bruce's skeleton had been discovered in 1818, it was re-interred with fitting pomp and ceremony below the pulpit of the new church. However, fortunately for Angus and his team, in 1891 the pulpit was moved back, and an inscribed brass plate inserted into the floor to indicate the exact position of the royal vault. This made access to Bruce's tomb much easier and quicker.

Angus had done a number of similar exhumations over the years, but the exhumation of King Robert was very special to him. When the day of this unique event arrived, he was almost overcome with the excitement and anticipation. A high canvas divider had been erected around the brass commemorative plate after the Sunday evening service. This divider, making the area of Robert's tomb private, was sufficiently large to allow ample working access to Angus's small team: him and Elizabeth and two of his most trusted staff still working out of his university office.

Angus was somewhat surprised with the easiness of removing the commemorative brass plate. The floor slab, although approximately two hundred pounds in weight, also lifted easily, and when placed aside, the oaken burial cask below was clearly illuminated by two floodlights Angus had arranged to shine down into the tomb. There was plenty of room to stand inside the sepulcher. After a few minutes of taking photographs, Angus descended into the tomb and stood beside the coffin, his heart racing, his body giving off small tremors and tiny beads of perspiration. Angus's moment of truth was soon to arrive.

Once again, Angus was surprised at how easily the oak coffin lid lifted, revealing the gold-colored shroud inside, still in excellent condition after almost seven hundred years, and just as Angus had anticipated from the drawings. Those above strained forward to get a better view as Angus took further pictures. Sewn into the shroud were heraldic and crest designs, some of which Angus recognized from the Bruce family memorabilia; the others he recognized to be associated with ancient Scottish royalty. During the last exhumation, this golden shroud had been completely unwrapped from Bruce's skeleton; in fact, a small part of the shroud had been removed with one of the king's toes and kept as a memento by one of the dignitaries of the town with access to the tomb. Now the shroud seemed just partially wrapped around the skeleton, giving direct access to the skeleton lying below. Angus had fleeting thoughts of someone else accessing the tomb since the last exhumation, but those thoughts quickly disappeared as he continued with the task at hand. The excitement of all those present now seemed tangible. Angus carefully rolled back the shroud.

As Angus slowly exposed Bruce's skeleton, it became obvious the skull had been slightly moved. He expected this, as skull measurements had been taken during the 1818 exhumation. From these measurements, sculptors in later years were able to accurately create the many monuments in his likeness. The broken rib cage was also expected; so far all had gone as anticipated. Upon revealing the lower arms and hands, Angus let out an exclamation of surprise and astonishment at what lay revealed before him.

"I knew it—I knew it," he exclaimed out loud. "Here is the sign of Bruce, and here is what we have searched for all these years!" He stood back a little, allowing all present to see as he pointed dramatically to the position of the skeletal hands and wrist bones.

"They have been moved from the clasped-hands praying position you can see in these drawings," continued Angus, now visibly shaking a little.

Sure enough, the left hand was turned palm down in a cupped position, and the right hand was curled in a closed-fist position resting inside the outstretched left hand. A piece of faded parchment paper was gripped in the right fist.

"Can't you all see?" continued Angus. "Surely our search is almost over if we can read the signs!"

Everyone just looked down, bewildered by this sudden turn of events. They knew nothing of the mentioned signs.

"Angus, please enlighten us," said Elizabeth.

"Remember what Doctor Yin said was written on the parchment paper in the silver casket under the tomb of Emperor Zeng?" he asked.

But of course no one knew about the talk Angus had with Dr. Yin.

Angus steadied himself, looked into the eyes of those waiting above with bated breath, and emotionally repeated Dr. Yin's words: "Scots will only rule their homeland after the clenched fist of Bruce rises again."

Total silence descended. All clearly appeared deep in thought as each made his or her personal conclusions.

Eventually, Elizabeth spoke, "Angus, are you going to read the parchment paper?"

Angus seemed to be in a trance, spellbound at this latest discovery. After a few moments, he leaned forward, carefully removed the parchment, and unrolled it for all to see.

The words, written in Old English script, were quite legible and read: "Seek below the mason's mark, and a resting place will be revealed."

No one present seemed to immediately make sense of these words, but Angus smiled with inner contentment. He knew where and why and when. Elizabeth knew from experience it was a smile of understanding and awareness; he had new secret knowledge.

Angus took a few more photographs, left everything as it was when he first uncovered Bruce's skeleton, raised himself out of the open tomb, and stood in a triumphant, elated stance before his friends and colleagues. He stood in silence for a minute or so and then in a firm and resolute voice said, "My friends, we must return another day to complete the work at hand."

That evening, Angus held a meeting in his office to which all those present in the abbey were in attendance.

"This afternoon, you all witnessed a most unique event, which I ask you all to keep secret until I can reveal, after permission from the relevant authorities, the result to the general public," requested Angus firmly.

All present nodded in agreement. Everyone now seemed to be in an increasing state of anticipation. What more could there be—what other secrets were still locked within the ancient tomb, and what relevance did this all have to Angus's mission to find the Stone of Destiny? Could he be near to fulfilling his lifelong vision?

"Friends," continued Angus, "for many years, I have believed there existed another casket buried at or about the same time as the casket containing King Robert's heart in Melrose Abbey. I now believe that casket lies buried under the coffin you all saw this afternoon."

All were silent until Elizabeth asked Angus, "What leads you to this new conclusion?"

Angus, with both hands open, shuffled a little from side to side, leaned forward, and continued in a slightly raised voice.

"The casket I examined at the Po Lin Monastery certainly used to contain some tokens or coins, which I believe will assist us in solving the mystery of the Stone of Destiny's whereabouts. I also believe there exists another casket brought back to Scotland from the crusades, along with King Robert's remains, similar to the one I saw at the monastery. It is my instinct that casket was buried here in Dunfermline Abbey by monks of the Benedictine order. I believe the same order of monks hid the original stone before the first King Edward could carry off a replacement to London. The bogus stone is now lying in Edinburgh Castle beside the Scottish crown jewels. We must lift the coffin of King Robert and look below."

"Could we borrow one of the University Medical School's computed tomography or X-ray machines to look down through the coffin and skeleton and see images of any casket lying below?" asked one of Angus's assistants.

"No and for just one very simple reason," answered Angus. "The coffin is lined with lead and the lead will prevent x-ray penetration."

Everyone remained silent and attentive.

"We must lift the coffin and see what lies beneath. That will take time and the know-how of others and must be done in complete secrecy. Does anyone have any practical ideas?"

"The police, when they retrieve DNA from a buried body, get the gravediggers to rig some sort of lifting equipment," ventured one of Angus's younger assistants.

"Good thinking," remarked Angus in genuine approval. "We must contact the police and ask them to help at the earliest opportunity! We have no time to waste."

Angus asked all present to again swear to secrecy and asked them meet at noon in the Abbey in two days' time. Two days would be sufficient time to make the necessary arrangements with the police and abbey authorities.

"All will be revealed then!" was Angus's optimistic parting comment.

All was in place to commence the coffin lift just after noon on the arranged date. Two gravediggers had earlier rigged the lifting equipment over the coffin and instructed Angus's party on how to safely use it. Two burly policemen stood guard at the entrance to the crypt. Soon the slow lifting process commenced.

"Stop the lift after twelve inches, and I can use this fiber-optic scope to scan beneath. If I see anything of interest, we can then continue the hoist," said Angus, visibly excited.

Slowly the lead-lined coffin rose into better view. After a few minutes, Angus called a halt. There was little space to maneuver, but Angus on hands and knees beside the visible portion of the coffin maneuvered the fiber-optic scope into position. A silence descended upon the scene. All those above waited anxiously, hoping to hear or see some positive sign.

The muffled voice from below gave off hope and anticipation.

"I can see a cloth-covered package about the size of a soup bowl. We will have to raise the coffin further to allow me to retrieve the package using the fish gaff I brought in case such a situation arose," said Angus, visibly elated at this find.

"The hooked end of the expanding gaff should be sufficient to snag the cloth and allow us the leverage to retrieve the package undamaged," explained Angus, flushed with excitement and personal satisfaction. "Elizabeth, bring the salmon gaff from my car while we continue the lift a few more inches."

Minutes later, Elizabeth arrived with Angus's fishing gaff. Angus joked he last used the gaff to land a rather nice spring salmon earlier in the year. "Maybe this 'fish' is not as large as that salmon," joked Angus, "but the package will hopefully prove greater in value and historical significance.

Gaff in one hand and optic scope in the other, Angus set about carefully retrieving the package. Angus feared the hook point might penetrate the package covering, so he employed a scooping action to work the package toward his eager hands. After a few minutes, the package came into view. Angus, bending over further, was able to grasp the package, and then he lifted it triumphantly above his head.

Placing the package on the altar top so all could see, Angus took a few more photographs from different directions and then spoke to Elizabeth in a cracking voice.

"Elizabeth, you have shared your life with me all these years. Now let me share this special moment with you: please unwrap the package.

Elizabeth stepped forward with moist eyes betraying her feelings and started to unwrap what appeared to be a muslin cloth from around a square, solid object. It was her turn to feel all the emotion of a lifetime's work coming to fruition. Elizabeth realized only she could possibly share the torment and anguish racing through Angus.

Elizabeth proceeded with much care and concern, and soon a box lay exposed for all to view. The metallic box was similar in color to tarnished silver and was eight inches long, four inches wide, and about two inches deep, having a lid slightly raised at each corner.

"Let me take some photographs before we attempt to open it," said Angus, laying a twelve-inch ruler beside the casket for comparison.

"Okay, go ahead, Elizabeth. Raise the lid if you can," said Angus when he was done photographing.

"I think you should, as the contents may make valid much of your life's work," replied Elizabeth.

"No, you have been with me all the way, and you are more deserving," answered Angus with an anxious but loving smile.

Elizabeth did as asked. The casket lid lifted with a soft grinding sound, quite clear for all to hear—a sound all present hoped was last heard hundreds of years ago.

Angus stared into the box for a few seconds, took Elizabeth's hands in his, raised them to his lips, and with a tremor in his voice said, "By opening this box, you have revealed much of the secret we have sought these past many years."

Angus turned the casket onto its side, allowing all those assembled to gain a better view of the contents. Inside stood a line of what should have been nine coins, but the middle three appeared to be missing. A small piece of marble-like stone lay between the row of coins and one side of the casket. Total silence descended over the scene, each person's mind racing with many questions. The calm and collected voice of Angus brought all back into the present.

"I believe the three coins or tokens missing from this casket were at one time inside the casket I viewed in the monastery. Imprints had been left on the recesses in that casket very similar to these in this casket." Angus paused a few moments for his words to be understood. He then continued.

"We must take photographs, get permission to remove the casket and its contents to a safe environment, and carry out a complete scientific study. We must also take impressions of all the contents. Can I have confidence in your abilities to keep all matters concerning this great find a secret?"

All present agreed to act in accordance with Angus's wishes.

Chapter 6

CORROBORATION

It took several weeks before Angus gained permission from the authorities to continue with his examination of the casket. Although paper documentation and photographs and measurements of the casket were important, it was the casket's contents that now became the focus of attention. The tokens were made of a bronze-like metal that had become quite tarnished with age. It required hours of meticulous cleaning before the symbols on both sides of the tokens were clear enough for molds to be made. It was Angus's intention to make clear replicas of the tokens, thus keeping the originals free from the wear and tear of continuous examination. The originals were kept undamaged in a secure safe.

Angus had three sets of the six tokens copied in silicone plastic material, along with three copies of the marble-like stone. When all the molding work was completed, Angus ordered the molds destroyed. Now he could set about a more detailed examination of the tokens, try to make sense of the strange markings, and most importantly try to discover the whereabouts of the three missing tokens. Within a few hours, Angus knew he had taken on a formidable task. He realized he would have to recruit someone more able than he to decipher the symbols. The inscriptions on each token, although quite different from each other, clearly conveyed a meaning when viewed collectively. Interpreting these meanings would require help from experts in the field of cryptography. Finding the three missing tokens could prove to be the most difficult part of solving the whole mystery. Time was running out.

Ideally all should be solved before the coronation of the new Scottish king, thus re-establishing the ancient line of Scottish monarchy. This is what the majority of Scots had voted for in a referendum held only a few months ago. The re-establishing of a monarchy not only reconnected with ancient times but also emphasized a renewed identity within the European community. Many of the countries within the European community already had long-established monarchies as their heads of state. Their systems seemed to work, although the monarch was usually required to act in only an advisory role, although the incumbent could veto bills. Many Scots felt the opening of markets and trade to an independent legislation headed by Scottish monarchy, previously denied by the Westminster federal government, could only benefit the nation as a whole.

One side of the tokens depicted two hands from the wrist up, clasped in an upright position. This position of the hands appears in many paintings of religious persons kneeling while in prayer, but hieroglyphic-like symbols were inscribed beneath the wrists. The symbols on all tokens were different. On the reverse side of the tokens was the outline of an eye. This eye was inside a triangle and looked left to right on three of the tokens and right to left on the other three. Under the eyes was some form of numbering, which appeared to indicate the order of reading the hieroglyphics.

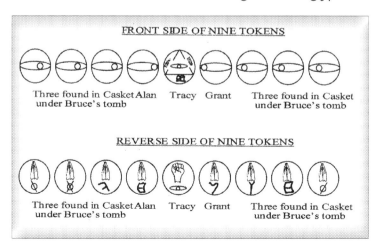

FRONT SIDE OF NINE TOKENS

Three found in Casket Alan   Tracy   Grant   Three found in Casket
under Bruce's tomb   under Bruce's tomb

REVERSE SIDE OF NINE TOKENS

Three found in Casket Alan   Tracy   Grant   Three found in Casket
under Bruce's tomb   under Bruce's tomb

Following a few days of quite unrewarding work trying to make sense of the engravings, Angus again found himself at a standstill. He realized, despite the possibility of compromising the secrecy, he needed more than ever to recover the three missing tokens. Without these, any translation of the symbols would be highly unlikely. Another exploratory hunt had to be started with maximum priority. For more than two weeks, everyone having knowledge of the casket and its contents puzzled over the best way to proceed. Even the most unlikely responses to the challenge were fully considered but eventually rejected.

"Angus, why not advertise in the media for anyone knowing the whereabouts or having any knowledge of the tokens to contact you immediately?" asked Elizabeth.

"But that would mean compromising our whole research. Everyone would want to know our reasons for advertising," replied Angus, surprised at what he thought was a naive response.

"Well, Angus, we have been here over two weeks working on a viable solution, and we are no further forward than when we started. What else can we do? Why not put my suggestion to a vote," said Elizabeth, a little surprised at her firmness. Angus, now faced with no other option, cautiously agreed.

The vote resulted in a unanimous win for Elizabeth's suggestion, and Angus redirected the group's efforts toward advertising. "There is no shortage of media within which we can advertise our search," said Angus at a meeting the following day." The problem appears to be choosing which medium will give the biggest impact and which will produce the response we need." Every person gave his or her analysis of the problem. Various proposed solutions were discussed; however, it was the proposal of young Jason Graham, an associate in the department of archaeology at the university, that most agreed was the best way to proceed.

"The most cost-effective method would be to construct an Internet site explaining our search regarding the tokens. There would be no need to say the reason for our search, just show a picture of the designs on the tokens that we already know about and ask for anyone with knowledge of similar tokens to contact us. The cost of producing such a site would be relatively little considering the vast exposure, and people could be directed to the site by our sending e-mails to all organizations with Scottish ancestral connections, medieval history, and anything Scottish in content. The St. Andrews Societies, Robert Burns Societies, Scottish Heritage Societies, and Masonic Lodges worldwide, particularly those adhering to Scottish Rite, would also be prime areas to target our enquiries," explained Jason.

"Well thought out," commented Angus. "Does anyone else have any other viable options?" he added.

"We could run adverts in the local and international editions of *The Scotsman* newspaper and have the BBC radio service broadcast a short program describing the nature of our quest without giving away too much information," stated Elizabeth. Once again, all agreed Elizabeth's plan was feasible and not too costly. Angus said he believed Historic Scotland had funds available to underwrite such things as advertising and the production of infomercials, but they would have trouble getting the funding without complete disclosure.

"Let's give all these suggestions a try," conceded Angus. Then he continued, "I have been given some discretion regarding use of funds for archival research. I am sure the director of Historic Scotland will also authorize use of funds at his disposal once I brief him on the project's progress. After all, he did authorize the exhumation of Bruce's tomb, and this is directly tied to what we discovered there," he added with an eager and confident tone.

All present nodded in agreement. Each left Angus's office tasked with contacting the various agencies they hoped would help find the missing tokens.

Hopes of a quick solution soon faded. Days passed into weeks with only a few replies to all their advertising. Although most of the responses were from people genuinely believing they had tokens similar to those described, none attracted Angus's attention as being of any great value. Certainly none of the samples or photographs submitted to Angus's office satisfied the medieval timeline or related to similar relics from the early Crusades era.

Chapter 7

COMING TOGETHER

"Hey, Tracy, what's all this about, you being Scottish and all that?" inquired the chief instructor of Qatar Air Academy. The school was situated near the city of Doha, a few miles inland from the south shore of the Persian Gulf.

"Let me see," said Tracy, taking the crumpled, week-old copy of *The Scotsman* newspaper from her boss's hand.

Tracy read the article regarding the tokens. Time seemed to stop as she remembered her crash into the South China seas so many years ago and the grief that haunted her ever since. She regularly remembered the token found within the casing of her smashed aircrew watch, now lying at the bottom of her jewel box. She had often tried to throw the token away and also throw away that part of her life she very much regretted. All those feelings and memories came flooding back as she read the article. She instinctively knew her token was one of the three Angus wished to locate—the one found inside her damaged aircrew watch returned to her by Davy Jones while she recovered in the Hong Kong military hospital.

Lieutenant Tracy E. Dunbar had resigned her Royal Navy commission less than one year after the accident during which the life of her Observer Lieutenant Kenny Adams had been so tragically lost. She had visited Kenny's widow, Kate, and her three young children at their home near Yeovilton Air Station only three months after Kenny's death. She had been overcome with the familiar survivor's guilt and vowed she would never put herself in a similar position again. Against the advice of her many pilot friends, she resigned and spent six months at her parents' home, secluded from the world at large and considering her new circumstances and less-than-clear future. The only naval person she had kept in touch with during those months was her one-time lover and the air traffic controller the fateful night of her accident, Don Stevens. She and Don eventually married, but things did not work out, and they divorced after five years of strained marriage; they had no children. Tracy then worked a number of administrative secretary jobs, but eventually the flying bug took over again. She completed a flying instructor course, was hired by Middle East Airways, and these past five years found working and living in Doha pleasant and rewarding. However, fate seemed to be pointing her toward her homeland. Tracy did what Angus's article requested. After her token had been photographed from both sides, she sent the photographs to Angus and included her contact particulars. She described how she had obtained the token and how she recollected some of the inscriptions resembled some of the insignia sewn onto her father's Masonic apron.

Life for the aging golfer Grant Sinclair had changed dramatically since he finished fifth in the Mission Hills Open Golf Tournament. Not only did his prize money of $380 thousand ensure him financial stability over the next few years, but finishing fifth also ensured invitations to other tournaments. He did not have to go through the qualifying rounds to ensure playing in the four-day tournaments. Over four years of tournament playing, Grant had never gained another fifth place. He had managed to survive reasonably well on winnings but usually finished in the bottom half of the competitors. Grant had the token left by Ah Ying mounted within a silver collar and suspended on a silver necklace, which he wore as a lucky icon in tournaments. He had never forgotten Ah Ying or the dreamlike night with her years ago, during which he had experienced all he could ever want with any woman. He became exceedingly superstitious and yearned for Ah Ying's caddie experience whenever he played competitively. Grant kept up his association with what had now become the Hong Kong Golf Club. When approached to join the teaching staff of the club, he readily accepted. Some years before, he had gained the necessary qualifications and now felt more content not having the strain of playing each week to maintain an acceptable income. A year after joining the club staff, Grant renewed his friendship with Julia, another golf instructor employed at the club's downtown Deepwater Bay facility. After a whirlwind romance, they married. Both now lived comfortably in their apartment at Tsuen Wan, happy with their stable financial situation and their positions on the staff, and they looked forward to many happy years instructing at the club before retirement.

Grant regularly attended the monthly meetings of his Masonic mother lodge, Western Scotia. These were held in Zetland Hall in the mid-levels of Hong Kong Island. He and Julia regularly attended the lodge's many social functions, made many new friends, and he accepted a lower-level officer position on the lodge organization board. It was during one of these board meetings the master of the lodge brought everyone's attention to a circular letter, a copy of the one Angus had sent to the Grand Lodge for circulation. After the letter had been posted on the lodge main notice board, the contents created much speculation among the members. During the meeting, Grant's hand seemed to habitually grasp the necklace he routinely wore, but he said nothing. His mind now reverted to memories of Ah Ying. He remembered both his good fortune when wearing the necklace and the handwritten note left by Ah Ying before he had woken up that memorable morning. He had memorized the words in her note and mused over them many times. The note said, "Keep this token. Treasure its yet-to-be revealed meaning and return the good fortune that will surely follow." Good fortune had certainly followed Grant. During the rest of the meeting he seemed to slip into a far-off dream, but before leaving that night, he made a photocopy of the letter for his more careful reading at home.

"What are you reading, dear?" asked Julia.

"It concerns something that happened to me some time ago that helped me get where I am today. It even helped us meet and live here and enjoy such a great and fulfilling life together," replied Grant.

"Is it something you would rather keep to yourself?" asked Julia. "I would respect you wanting to keep things that way, but you know we have always been open and supportive of each other. It would worry me if I remained unaware."

Grant knew Julia well; he knew she would feel quite rejected if he did not confide in her the story about the necklace he wore so often but never talked about. She knew he was superstitious about wearing the necklace, but many golfers were just the same. Even the great Tiger Woods always wore red clothing the last day of any tournament.

"Well, dear," began Grant, "it's a long, very personal, and unusual story, and I should have been more open with you about things that happened to me the day I finished fifth at Mission Hills. There were events I still wonder over, events which at the time were surreal and bizarre, but events that shaped my life from then till today."

He spent the next hour or so telling about those wondrous days, but even so he was economical with the truth. He did not relate anything about the very personal situation he and Ah Ying shared the last evening of the tournament.

"So what are you going to do regarding the request in Gillespie's letter?" inquired Julia.

"I guess we should let him know about the token within my necklace, take some photographs, and send them to him," replied Grant.

Within a few days, pictures followed their email to Angus. Grant and Julia waited curiously for a timely reply to their response.

Since the first Hong Kong and Shanghai Bank building opened in l865, that bank has dominated the Far East banking world. The new bank building completed in 1985 was at that time the most expensive building in the world. Shortly after the building was occupied, Alan Stewart, also known as Aux Marine Police Inspector Stewart, arrived on transfer from Scotland as the bank started to greatly expand, taking over other banking institutions worldwide. In the late 1990s, many staff transferred to the Hong Kong and Shanghai Bank's other large offices in Singapore due to the pending uncertain status of Hong Kong when the colony returned to mainland China in 1998.

Despite the uncertainty, Alan decided to remain in Hong Kong, a decision considered a career risk. After an uncertain period regarding the bank's future, the bank prospered greatly, as did Alan. He quickly climbed up the corporate ladder, mainly due to many of his seniors transferring out of Hong Kong to Singapore, and after a few short years, Alan found himself acting first as vice president of the bank and then taking over the president's position. Many of his staff regarded his rapid promotion as a well-deserved reward for his faith in the position of the bank and his faith in Hong Kong's future.

Alan took early retirement. After a round-the-world cruise, he finally set up a retirement home in the small Scottish town of Blairgowrie where many other Hong Kong bankers had retired and settled into a pleasant and agreeable lifestyle with his Chinese girlfriend of six years. Alan had never married, although he had many opportunities to do so. He and his girlfriend, a lovely, slim, tall northern-Chinese woman called Adith, were to all intents and purposes leading a happy married life, and both seemed happy to have things remain that way. Both soon became well integrated into the local community and became respected members of the local golf club, playing at least twice a week and attending most of the club's social functions.

"Winners of this year's mixed foursomes: Alan Stewart and his partner, Adith Ng," called the competitions secretary at the golf club's end-of-year awards dinner.

Alan and Adith went up to the presentation dais to receive their over hundred-year-old silver trophy, to the generous applause of all present. Adith's spectacular improvement in local golf tournament scores that year had made her quite in demand to play for the ladies team in interclub matches. She certainly looked the part and had a smooth-flowing golf swing much envied by other ladies less new to the game. But there was something mystifying about Adith, as she projected an air of secrecy about her past life. No one, even Alan, really knew about her life in northern China, and she never kept in touch with any of her family, if indeed she had any. Many of the ladies believed Adith must have played before, but where? The local golfers weren't sure of how many golf clubs there were in northern China, and Alan confirmed she had not played in Hong Kong. Then there was the mystery of her speaking perfect English with hardly any accent, something quite unexpected. She certainly attracted much speculation about her life before meeting Alan. Maybe she liked her life history to remain mysterious.

Alan had become an enthusiastic member of the local historic society. He had invited another member of that society, Ian McIntosh, and his wife, Fiona, to attend the awards dinner, so it was natural their conversation should turn to events of local historic interest.

"Did you hear the original foundations of Scone Abbey have been found and are shortly to be excavated?" inquired Ian.

"No, I have not heard," replied Alan.

"Well, there was an article in last week's *Scotsman* newspaper. You could look up the article on the newspaper's website," replied Ian.

"How interesting, was there any mention of Boot Hill or the ancient crowning ceremonies carried out there?" inquired Alan, his interest now rising.

"No, I don't think so. But you know Scone is only ten miles from here. Maybe we could arrange a society visit to see an ongoing excavation."

Alan nodded in agreement and promised to contact the public relations staff of Historic Scotland.

The next day, Alan looked at the Historic Scotland website. As expected, the information about Scone Abbey made headlines on the site's first page, which he read carefully. The article was really like a brief press release but even so, had gained much interest among local amateur historians. Many questions about the excavation work were published in the "Question and Answer" section. Alan printed out most of the article with a view to giving a presentation at the next society meeting. It was then he noticed an article published in the "Other News" section of the site that really caught his attention, made his heart race, and took him back to one dark night in Mirs Bay, just north of Hong Kong.

That article was the request by Angus Gillespie for anyone having information about tokens similar to the one pictured in the article to contact him. Alan clearly remembered the bizarre fashion whereby he came by a similar token during one of his marine Police patrols in the mid-1980s. He had often wondered about those strange circumstances and what the whole incident meant. All events during that dark night so long ago had meant nothing during the intervening years, but maybe now he was being given an opportunity to resolve the mystery. Alan decided to contact Angus at once, but not before looking closely at the token he knew still lay at the bottom of his Masonic regalia storage chest. This chest he had left locked since leaving Hong Kong shortly after retirement.

Alan contacted Angus at his office near Edinburgh City Chambers. A few days later, he arrived late one morning to show Angus his token and explain the circumstances of it coming into his possession.

"Good morning, Mister Stewart, it's a fine summer day to drive down from Blairgowrie," said Angus as Alan entered his office.

"Indeed, it is a very fine day. I hope I have something of interest for you," replied Alan.

"Let me hear the story about how you came by your token, and then we can have a close look at it. From the description you gave me, I feel you may well have one of the three tokens I and my staff have been seeking," continued Angus, finding it hard to visibly contain his excitement.

On completion of Alan's account of the happenings that took place that dark night in Mirs Bay long ago, Angus remained silent in deep thought for some time.

"You may be interested to know I have been contacted by two other persons who claim to have a token similar to this one," began Angus. He then continued, "These two persons have connections with Hong Kong about the same time you lived and worked there and received their tokens about the same time as you, so I think these circumstances much more than coincidence. We must try and get you three altogether, hopefully here in Edinburgh, to find out just what else you may all have in common."

Alan agreed to leave his token with Angus so impressions of both sides of the token could be taken and used for comparison with the tokens belonging to Tracy and Grant. Angus intended to return the original token to Alan when they met again. Comparison of all three tokens would hopefully indicate some path to follow during the days ahead leading up to the coronation.

Summers in Hong Kong can be very hot and humid. When the colony belonged to the United Kingdom, all expatriates working in Hong Kong were given vacation of four to six weeks' duration to get away from the oppressive conditions. For government personnel, it was mandatory vacation be taken out of the colony. That same policy had been retained after the colony had returned to mainland China rule and was still used by the Hong Kong Golf Club for expatriate staff vacation. Grant and Julia Sinclair were due to spend much of their yearly vacation with Grant's aging parents at their home near Carnoustie this year. They visited each of their respective parents during alternate years and had stayed some time with Julia's parents in southern England last summer. Carnoustie is less than two hour's drive south from the center of Edinburgh. When Angus heard Grant was going to be that near in midsummer, and knowing Alan Stewart was also less than two hours' travel away, it became most important for him to contact Tracy Dunbar and hopefully persuade her to also be in Edinburgh at the same time. Angus hoped they would be able to compare tokens, relate the circumstances that led to each obtaining their individual tokens, and exchange experiences, hopefully finding a common theme. Angus believed finding a commonality between all three to be a key factor in solving his search for Jacob's Pillow.

After numerous telephone calls and emails between Tracy and Angus, Tracy agreed to take advantage of her nonrevenue travel benefits with Middle East Airways and travel home to see her aging parents in the small village of Kenmore, located about seventy miles north of Edinburgh. She could easily drive south in little over an hour and meet with Angus, Grant, and Alan whenever it was convenient for all concerned.

Chapter 8

A MARK REVEALED

Angus, being somewhat a romantic at heart, dithered over what meeting date would be most favorable for attracting good luck and fortune. He favored the date of the first coronation the Stone of Destiny had not been used in Scotland, namely the coronation of Robert the Bruce held near Scone Abbey the March 25, 1306; however, it was now almost midsummer and waiting until the next year was out of the question. Angus eventually decided his meeting with the three token holders should take place on the July anniversary of Bruce's birth, July 11, 1274. He had thought about meeting on June, the anniversary of Bruce's magnificent victory over the English at Bannockburn in 1314, but Grant had indicated he was not arriving from Hong Kong till early July, so everyone agreed 2:00 p.m. on July 11 would be a good time to meet in Angus's office, situated close by old Parliament House, a few minutes' walk from Edinburgh castle esplanade down the renowned "Royal Mile" from the castle to Holyrood Palace.

Angus's old wood-paneled office was dominated by a paper-cluttered oak desk that faced the entrance. Behind his desk, a wide bay window let in shafts of early afternoon sunlight, and the narrow top panes of stained glass colored the light softly. The view outside was not overly restricted, and the outlook over picturesque Princes Street were envied by less fortunate tutors whose offices looked out over the cobbled High Street. His office was small and seemed even smaller with the addition of three leather wing chairs purloined from the dean's office to accommodate Angus's well-traveled visitors. Elizabeth had set up a round walnut table just inside and to the right of the entrance door. Today she intended to put it to use while serving coffee, tea, smoked salmon and cucumber sandwiches, and an assortment of biscuits, wafers, and scones covered with clotted cream. Devonshire clotted cream was one of Angus's weaknesses, but today was very special and Elizabeth thought, a good reason to spoil Angus and his guests. She also had at hand a bottle of well-matured sherry, another of port, and a half dozen Edinburgh crystal glasses laid out on one side of the serving table.

Alan and Grant arrived a few minutes early, and they had already been warmly welcomed by Angus and were comfortably seated when Tracy's light knock announced her arrival. She certainly gained everyone's attention as she, too, was warmly welcomed and settled herself into one of the high winged leather chairs. She still retained the stature and fullness of figure that many rejected suitors had found so alluring during her earlier life. She seemed more reserved than during her navy years, more at ease with her obvious attractiveness to the opposite sex, and she walked with an air of confidence and self-belief that had been missing for so many years after her unpreventable yet guilt-inducing accident. Elizabeth finished serving refreshments, cleared the table, and sat to one side of Angus's desk as he rose to speak.

"Tracy and gentlemen, I am most indebted to you all for affording me so much of your valuable time to travel and be here today. However, I believe your interest could be well rewarded, maybe not in monetary gain at this time, but certainly in terms of helping to solve one of Scotland's most intriguing mysteries and helping to legitimize an ancient tradition.

Angus paused. "Besides you, Alan, how acquainted are you all with our legendary Stone of Destiny?

"Is that not our ancient kings' one-time coronation chair?" queried Tracy.

"Yes," agreed Grant. "I believe we now have the stone back here on display with the Scottish crown jewels and quite right, too. It should never have been taken in the first place. At the very least, it should have been returned many years ago, especially after the Union of the Crowns following the execution of our Mary Queen of Scots. After all, her only son, James, was the first king to rule legitimately over both England and Scotland."

"Yes, Grant, you are quite right," answered Angus, and then continued. "I have good reason to believe the stone Grant refers to is totally bogus, and I believe I have sufficient proof. With your help, I believe we can find the original stone, and if successful, will re-establish our ancient coronation ceremony, a ceremony last performed some seven hundred years ago."

Angus remained silent a minute or so to let the full impact of his claim to be appreciated.

"Can I assume we are all here for some common reason?" asked Tracy. "Surely you didn't ask us here simply due to our Scottish birth. I know I have never met Alan or Grant before or even knowingly communicated with them. I think you should explain all and justify our presence here today," said Tracy, looking directly into Angus's twinkling and mischievous eyes.

"Yes! Surely you must be told," replied Angus. "Surely you must all be told about my work, my life's quest, my passion to find and reveal the truth. It has been many years since my beginning to seek out the truth. I will do as you ask and hope you become as excited and as passionate as I to know more of our past, present, and future and revel in the chance to reveal one of our nation's most guarded secrets—a secret entrusted to a few patriots over seven hundred years ago, a secret well-kept to this day, yet a secret which I believe we can now collectively reveal."

Angus picked up some papers from his desk, glanced through them quickly, and with a sigh of anticipated relief at sharing his secrets, began to speak. He was an experienced lecturer; he knew how to command attention, and he spoke with style and poise. He related the story of Jacob's Pillow, the legend of Robert the Bruce, his journeys all over to seek the truth, and the discovery of both caskets and the tokens found inside. He spoke of journeys to Hong Kong, the exhumation of King Robert, and his search for the missing tokens. Tracy, Alan, and Grant, hearing this for the first time, became spellbound as the story unfolded. They realized how involved they had been individually and knew instinctively that more was yet to unfold. They listened in surprise and wonder. What could all this mean to them personally, and what part did Angus foresee them taking in the months ahead?

The instant Angus completed his summary, he opened a safe attached to the side of his desk and took out a small locked steel-encased box and after opening the box, removed a small casket and placed it on the table.

"Here is the casket we recovered from under Bruce's coffin when we exhumed his tomb in Dunfermline Abbey a few months ago. You can see it is in excellent condition considering its age, which we estimate to be over seven hundred years, and you can see the six tokens inside still in the positions in which we found them. Three spaces remain empty. After looking closely at the photographs and the replica moldings you three have sent me, I am positive the tokens you have in your possession are indeed those missing from the casket. Now let me lay the tokens before you in the correct order and add your three tokens, and hopefully we will see a match between all nine and gain a bit more of the story they tell. I believe herein lies a message from Bruce himself and the ancient order of monks living in Scone Abbey during Bruce's reign. These monks, I believe, successfully hid the original Stone of Destiny from King Edward's advancing armies, and now, centuries later, we have been given signs that hopefully we can follow to recover the original stone.

"Do you have any questions at this time before we align the tokens?" asked Angus, giving time for each to fully appreciate the significance of finding the stone if Angus's convictions proved correct. A reflective silence descended over all.

"Why do you think only us three, out of all the world, received tokens?" asked Grant.

"Yes," jumped in Alan. "We three all seem to have been in or near Hong Kong when we received the tokens. Do you think that more by design than coincidence?"

"I feel there must be some connection through our common Scottish heritage and birth," added Tracy.

"And you, Alan, I know most likely to be a Mason of Scottish Rite, being so involved in the Hong Kong Shanghai Bank; maybe you, too, Grant. I know my father has been a long-time member of the Masons and continues to be a regular practicing master Mason within his mother lodge. Maybe this is the common link."

Silence reigned for a minute or so, allowing time for them to consider each angle.

"Angus, how do you know the tokens are in the correct order as we look at them? I appreciate the 'seeing eyes' look right to left on one side of Tracy's token situated in the middle, and other seeing eyes look left to right, but how do you know the correct order from the extreme left to the extreme right?" asked Alan.

"Good question, Alan," conceded Angus. "I, too, was worried about that very evident dilemma. However, when I tried to put the tokens back into the holding slots inside the casket, some of the tokens would not fit. It was not until I measured the thickness of each token that I noticed each was a few thousandths of an inch different in thickness from the others, and that particular token would only fit into one slot. You will notice, Tracy, the only slot your token fits is in the middle. And your tokens, Grant and Alan, only fit the slots to the right and left of the token belonging to Tracy. Does that answer your question, Alan?" concluded Angus.

"Yes, it does," answered Alan.

"Do any of these signs mean anything at all to you?" asked Grant. "Have you made any progress in deciphering what looks like ancient hieroglyphics running in sequence from token to token? Is there any connection between the objects depicted on both sides of the tokens? What does the symbol beneath the clenched fist on the back of Tracy's token represent?"

Before Grant's questions could be answered, Tracy added her own. "Is there any significance to the dates, at least I assume they're dates, along the opposite sides of the triangle on my token? What is the meaning of what appears to be a capital B?" Tracy pointed to a spot near the rim of her token on the same side where the numbers appeared.

Angus scribbled furiously for two or three minutes, writing short notes about the questions asked by Tracy, Alan, and Grant, along with a few notes of his own. He then carefully took an old leather-bound volume down from his bookcase and opened it to where a tattered bookmark protruded from the end of the book. Briefly making eye contact with each of his guests in turn, he locked the fingers of both hands together, placed them below his chin, and quietly spoke to them all.

"All the questions you have asked are quite valid and certainly warrant investigation to our utmost ability, but where do we start? How can we carry out this work and keep our efforts secret? Our research must remain hidden from the public eye and media scrutiny. If even a small part of our research is revealed, I fear the ensuing publicity would greatly hinder our research.

"Grant, you mentioned ancient hieroglyphics. Certainly the symbols appear to be of Egyptian origin, but this book here in front of us, a *Concise Study of Ancient Hieroglyphics*, does not show any similar markings. All hieroglyphics date from times well before the thirteenth or fourteenth century, some almost four thousand years before and certainly none after the fourth century BC. This period is long before our token inscriptions could have been made by the monks of Scone Abbey, if indeed they made them at all. For that reason alone, I feel we must look for another language from a different era and from a different civilization.

"I feel the clenched fist symbol is an indication to us here that now is the time to carry out our investigations and find the Stone of Destiny from clues we will be given along our path of exploration. Where these signs have come from, who has been responsible for allowing us access and giving direction toward solving the mystery will, for the time being, remain unknown. However, we all know the urgency for finding the original stone. Using the genuine stone would clearly legitimize, certainly from a traditional viewpoint, any future Scottish monarch coronations. The stone must be found in time, and the time for this first new era coronation is only a few months away."

Angus poured himself another cup of coffee and continued. "All the symbols you see inscribed below the clenched fists are also absent from this book. They do not appear meaningful to me at this time, and I am open to any suggestions regarding their origin. Maybe somewhere in your travels of the world, maybe somewhere in Hong Kong, even somewhere else here in Scotland, there are similar markings. Please scour the depths of your memories. Alan, Grant, try and remember anything similar you have seen during your Masonic meetings or written within your Masonic Rite documents and you, Tracy, maybe some inscriptions you have seen in ancient Middle East writings will come to mind.

"And now to the numbers—and here I do have clearer thoughts. The date 1274 is the year of King Robert the Bruce's birth, and 1329 is the year of his death at fifty-four years of age. These numbers standing alone appear as too obvious a clue. I believe there must be some code or cipher tied to those numbers. With regard to the capital letter B on the rim of Tracy's coin, again one can say it is no coincidence that B is the first letter of Bruce, but once again I feel that meaning too obvious. There must be more than this simple conclusion. I feel there is still something missing, something we are overlooking."

Almost two hours had passed since Angus had begun the narrative of his discoveries. The air of anticipation had been replaced with one of puzzlement and wonder, and naturally, doubt. Angus could see the confusion on each face, but he knew he had sown the seeds of hope and needed to take advantage while he had the chance. All the token holders were together for the first time, an occasion not easily repeated without considerable organization, considering the long distances some had traveled.

Angus asked Tracy and Grant how long they could remain in Scotland before returning to Qatar and Hong Kong. Tracy replied she could take an extended leave of absence if Angus needed her nearby. Once back in Qatar, she could always come at relatively short notice due to her position with the airline.

Travel for Tracy would not prove difficult. She would be able to use her travel benefits of nearly free flights, if there was space available on any of the London-bound flights. She was considered airline staff, and as such, she had unlimited access to nonrevenue flight tickets.

Grant's reply was not nearly so accommodating. He replied he could stay for almost two months by extending his annual six weeks' vacation and also taking another two weeks contract renewal leave, which he had accrued these past two years and not used.

Alan lived only an hour's drive north of Edinburgh, so availability would not be a problem

Angus was well pleased to have Alan, Tracy, and Grant available for at least the next eight weeks. He took down a sun-faded picture calendar from beside his bookshelf, turned over a few leaves, and left it open at August. "Can we all agree to meet here one month from today? Hopefully I will have some answers for each one of you during that meeting. If any of you have any thoughts that you think relevant, please be in touch by phone; I check my answering service frequently when I am out of town. Of course you can also contact me via email, which I access every day wherever I am."

The three guests lingered another thirty minutes, comparing stories and discussing each bizarre event that had brought them to Angus's office. Eventually everyone said their farewells after wishing Angus the best of luck in his endeavors and promised to keep in touch. Angus bade them farewell with a cheery smile and an optimistic, "Let the games begin!" But deciding where to begin would be the next crucial step needing immediate thought and action; and time was certainly not on his side.

Chapter 9

THE FACE OF BRUCE

Professor Ian MacDougall, dean of the department of modern and ancient languages at Edenside University, was certainly surprised to receive Angus's telephone call. He did not normally take calls himself; however his longtime secretary, Alice Gowans, knew Ian and Angus had been students together many years ago before going their separate ways and decided to put Angus through as soon as Ian was free to accept the call. Both had been successful in their chosen professions; both were well respected worldwide for their lectures, and both had successfully published several books. Alice exchanged a few words with Angus while Ian finished a conference call, and after some words of introduction, she put Angus through on Ian's private unlisted number.

"Long time, no speak!" quipped Ian when he knew Angus was connected. "What have I done to have the honor of your attention, Dr. Gillespie?"

"Nice to hear you still have the same sense of humor," replied Angus, who couldn't help smiling. "Ian, I have a great favor to ask of you, something I know you could be interested in helping me with, and something I know would give you great satisfaction and professional stature if you can solve the conundrum I have in store for you. Would you be willing to accept a challenge?"

"Well, let me hear what this conundrum is all about. I'm sure it must be challenging for you to decide it worthy of my examination. Please explain."

Angus's need for tight security had made him decide not to tell Ian the whole situation, especially how the puzzle was connected with his personal mission to find the Stone of Destiny. He only gave details of "some tokens found during an archaeological excavation" and then added a short description of the strange markings and respective locations.

"Those symbols," he said, "have inscriptions on them similar to other ancient script of Middle Eastern origin; however, I have already determined the markings are not associated with Egyptian hieroglyphics but are more similar to ancient Greek."

"I'm intrigued," admitted Ian. "But Angus, I know you must be holding back some information. You've only ever released precise, well-documented proofs, and there must be more to this than meets the eye." Ian paused a moment in thought. "Can you let me have a copy of the inscriptions on these tokens, or would you prefer we meet in person when you could show me the originals?"

"If I send you photographs of the tokens lying in the order we have found to be correct, could you give me some assessment of your findings within a few days?" inquired Angus. Then he added, "I will get the information to you via courier or secure mail later today."

"That would be just fine," replied Ian. "Please ensure you send them to my office here at Edenside University, marked for my personal attention. I am not too busy this week, so I should be able to find time to take at least a cursory look at your tokens. I will get back to you with my findings within four to five days. How does that arrangement suit you?"

"Just great," replied Angus. "And by the way, I feel the inscriptions could refer to an event that took place during the thirteenth to fifteenth centuries, maybe something to do with early Scottish kings, or even something religious concerning the Knights Templar and early Masonic ritual. But more than anything else, I feel the inscriptions could refer to the participation of Scottish nobility in Crusades to the Holy Land and religious artifacts associated with those Crusades."

"Okay, Angus, I will do my best. We will talk again toward the end of next week, and hopefully by then I should have some answers for you."

Immediately after Angus had said his good-byes, he packed the photographs and arranged for his preferred courier service to deliver them by hand to Ian at Edenside University that afternoon.

During the next few days, Angus took time to review all discoveries since meeting with Tracy, Alan, and Grant. He felt strongly that one of those three had a crucial piece of information if he or she could only recognize it. He had confidence in Ian MacDougall's ability as a renowned linguist. If anyone could make sense of the markings engraved on the tokens, it would be Ian.

Elizabeth, Angus, and his trusted staff members all agreed there must be some connection between the symbols—especially the symbol below the clenched fist on the back of Tracy's token, the digits relating to the lifespan of King Robert on the front and engraved on either side of the triangle, the forward-seeing eye, and the indented B on the outside edge of her token. All seemed to point toward another connection with King Robert.

Was the connection related to something else hidden within King Robert's tomb in Dunfermline Abbey? Did the monks of Scone Abbey confide in members of the Scottish Masonic Order, supposedly introduced by King Robert? Was there any involvement with the Knights Templar? The Templars supposedly came under King Robert's protection after many of their order had been hunted down in France and then brutally murdered en masse by papal orders in 1314. Perhaps when these questions were answered, the connection between them would point the way to the original Stone of Destiny.

A shrill ring from the office telephone abruptly roused Elizabeth, who had dozed in one of the office chairs. She stumbled up half asleep and answered the telephone.

"Doctor Gillespie's office, Elizabeth speaking."

"Hello, this is Fiona, Professor MacDougall's secretary, calling for Doctor Gillespie.

"Oh, yes," answered Elizabeth. "Angus is in the staff room. Please hold on a minute and I will get him, or would you prefer he called you back?"

"I will hold," answered Fiona. "Doctor MacDougall wants to talk with him as soon as possible."

Elizabeth told Angus about his waiting phone call. Visibly excited, Angus hurried along to his office, picked up the phone, and answered, "Angus speaking."

"Good morning, Doctor Gillespie, this is Doctor MacDougall's secretary. Please hold and I will transfer you to the doctor's desk."

Ian answered the call, and after a few inquiring good-natured remarks, came to the point of his call. "Well, Angus, you certainly managed to arouse my curiosity regarding the information you sent me. I have managed to make some semblance of logic out of the script lettering, but let me ask a few questions before I disclose my findings. At the moment, the translation I have does not seem coherent, but when I hear more about the script origins, I may be able to put things together in an understandable form.

You, of course, may see a correlation between the lettering and other historical events or geographical locations of which I am unaware."

"Yes," replied Angus. "That could well be the case. I am sorry I cannot, at this time, let you know the full circumstances; however, I will in due course. So what would you like to ask?"

"The fact you said there was no possibility these inscriptions were related to Egyptian hieroglyphics helped me immensely. At first glance, the inscriptions did bear some resemblance to the Egyptian script; however, with hieroglyphics off the table, I decided the inscriptions are not pictorial symbols but letters of either an ancient or disguised alphabet."

"Are you referring to the hands in prayer side of the tokens where we found the inscriptions read from left to right, according to the individual thickness of each token?" interrupted Angus.

"Yes, that is correct," answered Ian. "In your letter, you implied a connection between the token inscriptions and Crusades to the Holy Land, Scottish monarchy, and religion, and even the Masonic Order and Knights Templar. I presume you have not yet had the tokens carbon dated? From what you imply, I should not consider valid any answers that date the tokens and inscriptions being made after the fourteenth century. Is that correct?"

"Yes, that is correct," replied Angus. "Time is of the essence regarding my investigations, and carbon dating would have taken far too long. And of course, it would not be readily available without my compromising our whole investigation."

"I have been looking at languages and alphabets in use between 400 BC and the 1400s. Some of the characters on the tokens bear resemblance to several of the characters in at least two or three alphabets in use throughout the Middle East at that time. These alphabets were also used by various orders of monks and religious sects domiciled in Western Europe, including England and Scotland in post-Roman times. This use of the alphabets continued well after the Norman invasion in 1066, thus allowing secure communication in times of persecution, and one was supposedly used by Mary Queen of Scots as late as the sixteenth century during her incarceration at Queen Elizabeth's command."

"Yes, I knew about the notes Mary tried to smuggle out to her supporters, which, when found, led to her execution, but what was the language she used? I thought she only spoke French, Latin, and English, but was she not also competent in written Greek?"

"You are quite correct, Angus," replied Ian. "Remember, the language of the Scottish court was French in those days, as was the language used by the English monarchy, and it is here I have found a significant possible connection, but more on that later.

"I have presumed a direct substitution into the English alphabet from each token inscription; however, the problem is not just finding the correct language. The form of English being used during this time frame only had twenty-four characters, as 'i' and 'u' had not then been added to the alphabet we know today. Therefore a complete substitution may not be possible, and in the photograph you sent for translation, there is only one recurring symbol, thus adding to the obscurity. However, as the inscriptions were sufficiently similar to many of the letters of the Greek alphabet, I have concentrated my search on languages of Greek or Eastern Mediterranean origin. I believe I may have just, rather by good fortune than well thought-out research, stumbled on one obscure translation. With some imagination, that translation could fit most of your circumstances."

Angus was fascinated by his friend's news and glanced over to Elizabeth, who was listening in on the conversation. He asked Ian if he could record their conversation for quick reference purposes and hastily signaled Elizabeth to start the answering machine recorder when Ian gave his permission to record their conversation.

"Your news sounds exciting," added Angus. "Please enlighten me."

"The Euboean alphabet, a Western variation of the early Greek alphabet, was used up to a couple of centuries before the birth of Christ anywhere west of Greece, especially in southern Italy. An Eastern variant of this Euboean alphabet was eventually adopted in Athens. After Hellenism spread this alphabet to the vast Greek-speaking territories of the east Mediterranean, the original Western Greek alphabet became obsolete, and eventually the Eastern variation gave rise to the Old Italic alphabets, including the Latin alphabet," explained Ian. He paused to let Angus comment.

"Do you think the various monk orders of that time used that alphabet in their writings?" asked Angus.

"Yes, they did, and there have been some recent findings during the excavations of Cuma in 1992 validating that theory. However, what I find of more interest in view of the later time period you alluded to is yet another variation of the Western Greek alphabet." Ian paused again to shuffle some papers he was referring to and continued.

"Many religious orders were much persecuted between the twelfth and fourteenth centuries and even massacred, as was the case of the Knights Templar in the early fourteenth century. Normal written communication between the various abbeys and monasteries became very risky. Codes and ciphers were in common use to prevent the content from being interpreted by the rulers of the day if any letters were intercepted. Cistercian monks used a form of communication using an archaic variation of the Etruscan alphabet recently found to be almost identical to the western Greek alphabet. In recent years, that alphabet has been described as the Marsiliana abecedarian. I believe using this alphabet I can deduce a probable translation from your token inscriptions. I have used the left-to-right order of each separate inscription as you requested. This order, I understand, you deduced from the individual thickness of each token. Is my assumption correct?" inquired Ian.

"Indeed it is," answered Angus, "but can you share with me your translation over the phone?"

"Certainly I can, if you feel no security problems arise in so doing. It is really your call, Angus; I am not privy to all your deliberations."

"Go ahead," encouraged Angus.

"I will make use of the NATO phonetic alphabet; are you ready to copy?"

"Surely, go ahead," replied an enthusiastic Angus.

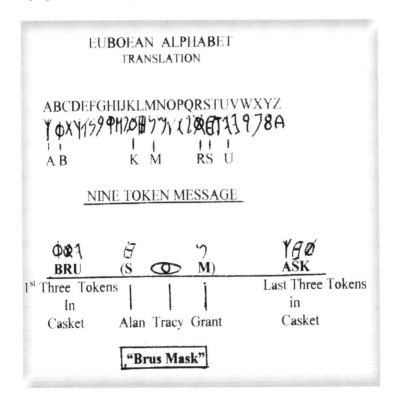

"The first letter is B-bravo followed by R-romeo and U-uniform and then S-sierra, that S being on the coin belonging to someone you called Alan. The next inscription on the smaller token belonging to someone called Tracy is not in the Marsiliana alphabet. The next letter is M-mike on the token belonging to someone called Grant, and then the remaining three letters are A-alpha, S-sierra, and K-kilo. Together, the tokens spell out 'Brus,' then the symbol on Tracy's token, then the word 'Mask.' Does this translation mean anything to you, Angus?"

"Well, Ian, yes it does! Something is ringing little bells in my mind right now. You have been of great help and you will be the first to know if your translation helps bring a satisfactory end to my speculation," answered a now thoroughly excited Angus.

"Please keep me informed of your progress. In the meantime, I will send you a copy of the alphabet and my translation for your records," said Ian before bidding Angus a cheerful farewell.

"Well, that was quite something. Would you not agree, Elizabeth?"

"Yes, Angus," replied Elizabeth. "I really think we are moving in the correct direction. Ian's results help greatly. What we must do now is discover how his translation can be applied to a real place or event. Surely someone we know would understand the meaning of Ian's translation. Who else may be able to provide some meaningful insight?"

"We need to get Tracy, Alan, and Grant together again as soon as possible," replied Angus. "I believe one of them unwittingly holds the key to revealing the message in Ian MacDougall's translation. I will contact Alan, as he lives the nearest and is already involved in his local historical society. I would like to hear his thoughts about the translation and discover more about his genealogy. I will also ask Tracy and Grant to forward their known genealogy. We may find a relationship between all three families dating back to, or even before, the middle Ages."

"Yes," replied Elizabeth. "That information would be of great assistance, but first we must wait for Ian's letter containing the message and translation to arrive. I think you will agree we need to wait a day or two allowing us to confirm the accuracy of the notes you made regarding your conversation with Ian. After all, they were written down from what you remember of the conversation, and at this stage we need to be absolutely sure of every fact."

"Indeed," agreed Angus. "It's been a most gratifying and rewarding day. Let's wait and see what tomorrow brings."

Chapter 10

ANOTHER MASK

The day Ian's letter arrived was a typical midsummer day in Edinburgh. A low-lying early morning mist hung over the city, reducing visibility, but by noon the sun had burned off most of the mist and a bright sun hung high in the azure sky. The barest wisp of wind made the castle esplanade streamers flutter, but the many international flags lining the length of Princes Street hung limp from their decorated flagpoles as the blue waters of the River Forth slowly emerged from below the low-lying mist. The sun had ascended high above Observation Hill when the mail arrived.

"Angus," called Elizabeth as she received the mail, "Ian's letter is here from Edenside. It's addressed to you, so I think it best you open it. I'm just your humble but interested secretary," she teased with the slightest of smiles.

Angus hurried in from the staff anteroom, took the letter from Elizabeth's outstretched hands, and quickly opened it, slightly tearing the envelope flap in his hurry.

"Dear Angus," began Ian's letter:

Please find enclosed the translation of the token inscriptions we talked about earlier. I have included the alphabet from which I made the translation. I hope you and your staff can make something more than I can of the eight letters which spell out "brus mask." Do keep me updated when able.

Yours,

Ian

Angus laid the letter flat on his desk, allowing both he and Elizabeth to examine the translation again.

After some deep thought, Angus turned to Elizabeth with an exuberant grin. "I really consider we are on the correct track; all the signs of being so are here before us. Although Ian could not see any association or connection, I believe I do."

After a short pause, he reached out to Elizabeth and grasped her hand, almost instinctively. "All along I have held that King Robert the Bruce, even from his tomb, has been trying to show us the way. The Bruce family originally came to Scotland not long after the Norman invasion of England in 1066. They were related to Norman the Conqueror, and the family name was adapted from the name of the town where the family originated and lived immediately before the Norman invasion. The name of that town is Brix or more commonly known as Brus. The word 'Brus' in Ian's translation makes perfect sense. Not only is that a direct connection to King Robert, but remember the language of both the English and Scottish Court was French in those days. Anyone writing Bruce in those days would have written 'Brus'!"

"Yes, yes, I see," replied Elizabeth. "That's quite logical when taken in context, but what about the word 'mask'?"

"Do you remember Doctor Lun Yin, the archaeologist to whom I talked regarding his visit to Rosslyn Chapel during a reception for him at the university almost a year ago? Remember as a consequence of that conversation, we traveled to Po Lin monastery on Lantau Island in Hong Kong only a few months ago."

"Yes, indeed I do," replied Elizabeth, "but where is the connection?"

"Doctor Yin was excited to see what we all consider a fake death mask of Robert the Bruce hanging on one of the inside walls of Rosslyn Chapel. He seemed to connect with Bruce when referring to the Yang Dynasty emperor installation ceremony and also referred to a stone. That stone he believed to be similar in purpose to that of our Stone of Destiny—it was used during Yang Dynasty emperor installation ceremonies. The supposed death mask is the connection and a very good one too. Maybe there was such a mask and the original has been hidden for many a year, maybe hidden along with the Stone of Destiny."

"But Rosslyn Chapel was not built till long after the death of Bruce. In fact, the early part of the chapel was not even started until 1446 by the second William St. Clair almost one hundred years after the internment of King Robert, so how could there be an original mask within the chapel confines unless it was added many years later? In reality, many of the carvings were still being collected until the late nineteenth century, and if that was the case regarding the reputed death mask, who added the mask and why?"

"Do you think there is any relationship between the symbol on Tracy's token and Bruce's death mask, genuine or false?" asked Elizabeth, now quite convinced there was some link.

"My dear, you are beginning to think along the same lines as I these past few months. However, there are too many gaps in my knowledge of the Knights Templar, the Scottish Rite Masonic Order, and even the involvement of King Robert himself in things of that nature, if indeed they ever took place during his tumultuous reign. Was he ever involved in Free Masonry? Was there any Knights Templar association with or without their protection from the Scottish crown during his time? And what if any, is the Bruce connection with Rosslyn Chapel? We know much said about Rosslyn Chapel is considered false. However, one of the ancestors of the St. Clair family, the family who started building the chapel, was Sir William St. Clair. Sir William was one of the Scottish nobles who accompanied Sir James Douglas carrying Bruce's heart on the crusade that ended tragically at the battle of Teba in 1330. That fact alone I feel carries great significance and needs further investigation, and I know exactly who can help us, namely Alan Stewart."

"Alan Stewart!" exclaimed Elizabeth. "The same Alan Stewart who met with us in these offices a week or so ago?" she questioned with a somewhat skeptical tone of voice. "What can Alan contribute? I cannot really understand your thinking, unless you know much more than I."

"Well, my dear, that indeed I do." And Angus started to explain.

"You know for some time now I have been looking into the backgrounds of Tracy, Grant, and Alan. I was hoping to find something common in their family history, their areas of interests, qualifications, where they went to school, travel experiences, anything tying them together in even the most tenuous of ways—anything that could possibly answer the question of why only these three received tokens. So far, I have been unsuccessful, but in carrying out this research, I gathered a great deal of information about all three persons, and in Alan's case there certainly appears to be a connection with Rosslyn Chapel—a connection possibly more important than I anticipated."

Elizabeth sat down, knowing from experience Angus would draw out the description of what he had learned. She had endured many mini-lectures when Angus tried to put in plain words some theory he thought well beyond her understanding.

She waited tolerantly for him to start. This was one time she certainly had more than a passing interest. Angus then spoke.

"Alan was born and raised in Roslin, a small town close by Rosslyn Chapel. Roslin has recently become quite famous due to the Roslin Animal Research Institute managing to clone the first animal, namely Dolly, a sheep raised on the institute premises."

Elizabeth nodded in agreement at the mention of Dolly.

"His father became town bank manager when Alan was attending the local school, and after Alan's father retired, Alan himself took over his father's position. Alan's father was a well-respected member of the community and was also a Mark Master Mason attending the local lodge meetings on a regular basis. Alan also became a mason in the same lodge and was active there as well as in the lodge he joined in Hong Kong. He remains active to this day within his local lodge based near his present home in Blairgowrie.

"Alan spent much of his childhood in and about Rosslyn Chapel, which was very much in disrepair at that time. He and his schoolmates spent many hours playing games in the chapel and exploring the various nooks and crannies, partly sealed catacombs, and crypts. If anyone knows the chapel intimately, that person would be Alan. He is very active in his local historic society and recently gave a series of lectures on Rosslyn Chapel, its history, its supposed secrets and myths, and its believed connections with the Knights Templar and ancient Masonic societies. It is that knowledge we must have him share with us, particularly the circumstances concerning a supposed Bruce death mask sculptured somewhere within the chapel sanctuary. Do you not agree?" queried Angus.

"Yes, I do agree," replied Elizabeth. "What are your intentions?"

"When I talked with Alan yesterday, I told him about the recent developments and Ian's translation. I asked him if sometime in the near future he could meet us here, hopefully along with Tracy and Grant if they are also available, and acquaint us with his obviously deep knowledge of the Rosslyn Chapel. This he has agreed to do whenever I can make the necessary arrangements, so we must move quickly."

Both Tracy and Grant arrived a few minutes late to attend the hastily called meeting. Also present with Angus and Elizabeth were Martin and Ena, two trusted members of staff made available to Angus by the university archaeological department.

"Thank you all for coming at short notice to attend this meeting," began Angus. "I think it a good omen you were all available at such short notice. I hope you will all be as excited as Elizabeth, Alan, and I are at the good news we have to tell you." Angus then related the events of the previous week and explained why he wanted Alan to talk about Rosslyn Chapel, while briskly distributing copies of the translation Ian had done.

"I do not wish to waste our time and energy chasing tenuous and unsubstantiated links to Rosslyn Chapel; therefore, I need your agreement to continue down this avenue of investigation. Please ask any questions you have as Alan progresses, and he will stop and respond."

Alan replaced Angus behind the oak desk, laid out a few papers before him, and started his presentation. "I am sure you must all be familiar with a book called *The Da Vinci Code* and a film of the same name released shortly after that book's publication," began Alan. He paused while those present indicated they had heard about the book. Tracy and Grant said they had also seen the film of the same name.

"Toward the end of both the book and the film, Rosslyn Chapel plays a significant, although brief, part. As a result the chapel has regained considerable worldwide interest—even celebrity, but I regret to say much said about the chapel, its history, its association with Knights Templar, Scottish Freemasonry, the Holy Grail, and so forth is very dubious. Much of the mystery and intrigue can even be considered a hoax. But let me better explain what otherwise appears to be a somewhat surprising and even unpatriotic statement.

"One theory concerning the chapel states the Stone of Destiny—along with the Holy Grail and other ancient documents, mostly concerning the legendary history of Freemasonry—are buried deep within the vaults under the chapel floor. This supposition is most unlikely and unsubstantiated. For example, let us examine the case for the Stone of Destiny being hidden there. Scone, where the stone was kept until King Edward carried off what he thought was the original stone, is some seventy miles to the north of Roslin. The stone is estimated to weigh three hundred and fifty pounds, so it is highly unlikely the monks reputed to have hidden the stone would not have found a suitable hiding place much nearer Scone Abbey. There also arises the problem of transporting such a visible and heavy object over such a distance without being seen in the face of an advancing English army. Most importantly, the fact remains that the building of Rosslyn Chapel was not started until more than one hundred years after King Edward I's army arrived in Scotland. This fact does not eliminate the possibility of the stone having been transported there many years later, as were many other artifacts. Artifacts and carvings were still being added to the chapel in the late nineteenth century."

"So you feel there is no chance the stone lies within or under Rosslyn Chapel's flooring?" asked Tracy.

"Exactly. However, saying so does not preclude my thinking there are signs and symbols within the chapel showing the way to find the stone. I sense, as does Angus, that persons willing and able to look into the minds of those ancient monks, or their successors, will think that way. And that brings me to King Robert the Bruce and his supposed death mask."

Alan paused a little to glance over the papers before him. After sipping from his soft drink, he continued. "Just about eye level on the wall of the retro-choir within the chapel is carved an image that bears a unique and mysterious inscription, which reads, 'The carving of the Death Mask of Robert the Bruce.' Underneath this inscription is added 'Robert the Bruce who was not only a Templar but the Grand Sovereign Grand Master of both the Military Order and the Masonic Guilds. His death mask is carved here.'

"These inscriptions are quite historically misleading, as nowhere has it been reported in any historical document that a death mask of Robert Bruce was made that survived the almost one hundred twenty years until the building of the chapel commenced in 1446. Also, never has it been claimed that Robert had connections with the Knights Templar or the Masonic guilds. It is often stated the Knights Templar came to Bruce's aid at the Battle of Bannockburn, during which the Scottish Army routed the much superior forces of King Edward. However, it is a well-known historical fact that most of the Knights Templar forces were wiped out on October 13, 1306, by the French king, reputedly carried out on orders from the Vatican. Incidentally, this event was the origin of the saying, 'Black Thirteenth of October.' The Battle of Bannockburn took place in June 1314, some eight years after the massacre, making it unlikely any Knights Templar were even in Scotland at the time, far less present at the battle. It may be wishful thinking, and in many ways quite romantic and idealistic, to think King Robert was all he was portrayed to be. However, I think it foolish and a waste of our valuable time to get overly excited about the hypothetical connection between our search and the supposed death mask of Robert in Rosslyn Chapel. Nevertheless, I must admit it somewhat more than a coincidence that Professor MacDougall's translation does refer to such a mask."

"So you think we are wasting our time looking for connections within Rosslyn Chapel regarding Bruce's supposed links to the

Knights Templar or the Scottish Rite Freemasonry?" asked Grant, sounding dejected.

"Well you could say that, Grant," replied Alan. "However, I do believe we must still examine some parts of the chapel regarding what we think is a symbol on the back of Tracy's token."

All present looked again at the illustration of Tracy's token lying before them. After a few moments of silence, Alan continued.

"From the depths of memory, I have been trying to recollect where I have seen such a symbol. I recall seeing a similar symbol somewhere on one of the inside walls when my school friends and I played at will in the uncared-for chapel. There were many old, disfigured, and even new engravings on the walls, but I believe I saw this mark there."

"What jolted your memory?" inquired Elizabeth.

"Again a coincidence, if you will, a coincidence only exposed this morning while I was looking over the translation. I believe this symbol is a Masonic mark; this I will explain later. My memory returned while taking a quick sideways look at the mark, it being turned ninety degrees to the right. It was then I perceived the mark as a monogram of the letters RB. I was thinking of Robert Burns, having recently been to a Burns Society meeting, but then it dawned on me those initials could just as easily mean Robert Bruce!"

MASTER MASON MARK

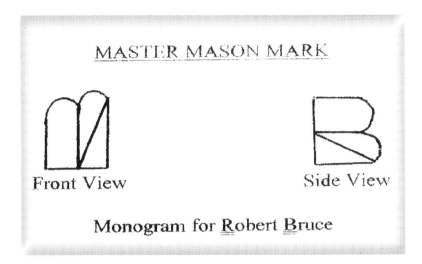

"So you now think there is a connection," said Tracy.

"No. Not a connection as such—but a sign showing a more valid direction for us to explore. Let me clarify. As most of you already know, I have been involved with Scottish Rite Freemasonry for many a year. My association with various lodges started when I was the local bank manager at Roslin, and after that I became an active member during my stay in Hong Kong. In recent years I have continued to be active in my local lodge at Blair, so I am well acquainted with the various traditions, workings, and degree levels that operate within the Ancient and Accepted Scottish Rite, to give the order its correct name. But you may ask, what has that to do with the mark on Tracy's token?"

Alan again referred to his notes before continuing. "There are three main levels of degree that anyone becoming a mason is obliged to work through and attain. Of course there are more than three, but it is the first three, and what some call a fourth, with which I think we should concern ourselves today.

"The first degree, called the degree of an entered apprentice, is the degree of initiation that makes one a Free Mason, whilst the second degree, called the degree of Fellow Craft, is an intermediate degree involved with learning. The third degree, called the degree of a Master Mason, is a degree one has to attain before being allowed to participate in most senior aspects of Free Masonry.

"The next degree and the degree that is most relevant to us here today called the degree of a Mark Master Mason, is sometimes called the fourth degree. This mark degree is conferred in a craft lodge and is seen as the completion of the Fellow Craft Degree. On completion of this degree, the recipient creates a sign 'mark' that is uniquely his. This mark is stamped onto his certification of Craft Master Mason and will be his and his alone for the rest of his life. Of course, his mark also serves as a form of identification within the organization."

Alan paused, allowing time for any questions and for his most attentive audience to assimilate all this new and mystical information. No questions were asked, and he continued.

"Master mason marks are a form of shorthand in place of a signature, just like people initial parts of a legal document instead of signing it in full. However, these Masonic fourth-degree marks are anonymous and cannot be dated. It would have been impractical for a working mason to initial every stone he worked, but some form of identification was required, as stonemasons were paid by the number and the quality of stones completed. Simple geometric marks were the answer. On completion of his apprenticeship, every stonemason would take a mark to be his for the rest of his life. After stonemasons completed the dressing of each stone they worked, they carved their mark on the hidden side of the stone. Thus, when the stone was laid in place, the mark was inside and hidden from view. Naturally nobody would wish the wall, pillar, arch, or statue to be defaced by any visible mason marks. The one exception appears to have been that the master mason in charge of the overall work was permitted to engrave his mark in a discreet position, usually high up out of obvious view. This mark indicated the work had passed the master mason's examination."

Grant asked, "So you think the symbol on Tracy's token is the mark of a master mason involved in building Rosslyn Chapel?"

"Yes, I do," answered Alan. "Furthermore, provided we can locate this mark, I feel we may find other things of interest; of course, I cannot guess what they might be."

The silence that fell over the room seemed loud after so much startling information. Alan took a seat, as the others were clearly deep in thought, turning over their own interpretations of all the clues before them. After a while, Angus stood up. Looking intently into each face, he saw bemusement, but he also saw a willingness to learn more. "There is much attributed to Rosslyn Chapel, a good deal of which can be entirely refuted," he began. "Legends point to artifacts hidden within the chapel's vaults. These legends maintain that the chapel contains hidden clues to finding even better hidden treasures. These treasures are reputed to include the Holy Grail, whatever that may be, the Ark of the Covenant, the Nasorean Scrolls, the embalmed head of Jesus Christ, treasures of the Knights Templar, and even the real Stone of Destiny. So what can we now base our hopes upon?

"We know of a supposed death mask, genuine or copy, placed in the chapel in relatively recent years. We know of marks carved on the chapel masonry, perhaps similar to the symbol on Tracy's token. And I know of one other oddity I have not yet conveyed to you; this fact I think worthy of consideration even though it may be pure coincidence."

He paused as all present looked up at him expectantly.

"I have recently completed some research into the inscriptions on the headstones in the Vault of the Quire within the chapel. One inscription reads, 'Alexander Earl of Sutherland, great grandchild to King Robert the Bruce.' With yet another connection to King Robert, I feel we must continue our search within the chapel.

If we look there with due diligence and attention to detail, my instinct tells me we will be well satisfied."

A few days passed while Angus made arrangements for himself, Elizabeth, Tracy, Grant, and Alan to make a private visit to the chapel. He received approval from the Director of Historic Scotland to conduct a personal search for the mark and to view the death mask carving. Best of all, the director also informed the curator of the chapel that Angus should be allowed to make his investigations when the chapel was closed to the public. Angus greatly appreciated receiving the director's help and promised to personally keep him informed of any relevant findings.

Angus and Elizabeth arrived a few minutes early the day he had arranged to visit Rosslyn Chapel and meet with Henry Bain, the chapel curator. Tracy had made arrangements to delay her return to Qatar and had traveled to Roslin with Grant, and Alan joined them a few minutes after noon. Even during the year or so since Angus's last visit to the chapel with Dr. Yin, many renovations had taken place. A new, unusual protective covering had been erected over the old roof to safeguard the chapel from the oft-dismal Scottish winter; much cleaning of the building stonework had been completed; and a visitor's center and gift shop waylaid visitors both coming and going. Since *The Da Vinci Code* had been published, and then produced as a film, visitor numbers had increased more than a thousand fold, and for that reason it had become necessary to make the chapel much more visitor friendly.

When all had gathered in the visitor center entrance hall and introductions were complete, the curator asked what he could do to help, though he politely avoided asking about the circumstances that related to their inquiries.

"We are interested in looking at what is believed to be the Bruce death mask sculpture and examining any ancient stonemason marks in the vicinity of the mask," replied Angus.

"That I can easily arrange," promised Mr. Bain. "I will show you to the general area and agree to you examining whatever seems to be of interest." Bain paused a few seconds and then said, "I will lock the entrance door when I leave to give you privacy. If you need anything, just call my mobile phone."

"That would be just fine," replied Angus. Then he added, "Your help is very much appreciated."

"Thank you," responded the curator. "Just follow me."

The curator turned and started walking toward the east end of the chapel; Angus and his group followed close behind. After passing close by the famous Apprentice Pillar, they all stopped opposite a wall adorned with a number of sculptures and small statuettes.

"Gentlemen, here is the object of your inquiries," said the curator, pointing at a sculpture set at about eye level on one of the east-wing walls. "Can I offer any other assistance?"

After Angus politely answered, "No thank you, you've been a great help," the curator turned and left in the direction of the visitor center.

Angus closely examined the mask sculpture, referring frequently to some written notes. Seemingly satisfied, he turned to his fascinated followers.

"I have no doubt this supposed death mask sculpture was not completed until many years after the death of King Robert and placed here long after the chapel had been completed. That fact alone makes me somewhat wary of the validity of any clues we may find here in our quest for the Stone of Destiny."

"So you think this mask is a fraud?" asked Tracy.

"Not quite. I do think it genuine, but it was made hundreds of years after King Robert's death and therefore not valid regarding the timeline we are interested in," replied Angus. "Let me explain more.

"Never during the years from King Robert's death up to the finding of his tomb in the 1800s has there been any mention of an existing death mask. If there was one made shortly after his death in 1329, it must have survived for well over one hundred years from the date of his death to about 1446 when the building of this chapel commenced. It would have then been sculpted into stone and placed in the retro-choir. It is not clear if the sculpture is claimed to be the actual death mask or if it is a copy. Examination of information on Robert I's death and burial confirms that no one had previously mentioned the existence of a death mask. The earliest known death mask in Europe is that of Edward III, who died in 1377; however, death masks did become common in the fifteenth century. How could the existence of such a significant artifact have remained unmentioned and unnoticed for so long? Prior to 1993, no references to a death mask or any connection between that mask and Rosslyn Chapel could be found. Many writers during the past four hundred years wrote and described the chapel, but none, as far as can be ascertained, have made any suggestion that Scotland's most famous monarch had been immortalized within Rosslyn Chapel." Angus paused.

"So why do you think this sculpture is here? What is its significance, if any? Why have we gathered here if you think this sculpture is a fraud?" asked Alan.

Angus walked a few paces in front and away from the sculpture. "I believe we have been guided by person or persons unknown to this mask, not for what it is or signifies, but because of its position here in the chapel. It is here we are being asked to look further, to expand our search for other signs. I believe that sign to be a master stonemason's mark, similar to that mark on the back of Tracy's token, a mark that Alan has already shown to be an anagram or the initials RB. That mark I believe to be near this mask facing us."

"But looking in close proximity to the sculpture, I can see many inscriptions; some look old, some new. How can we determine those that are genuine, let alone those relevant to our search?" exclaimed Alan.

Angus stood back a little and looked closely at the wall. "Some of the marks in Rosslyn Chapel cannot be accepted as being marks of stonemasons for several reasons. First, many are not discretely hidden away or in high positions. These marks are a form of graffiti added over the years for the same reasons that people carve their names or initials on trees. These are fairly easy to identify from their rough appearance—obviously not the product of a mason's maul and chisel. Mason marks are deeply incised to prevent them from being erased and are made with clean, angular lines. We must separate the chaff from the wheat, so to speak."

Angus tilted his head back and pointed up toward the top of the stone wall facing him, saying, "There is a lighter-colored stone up near the ceiling with some form of engraved marks showing. Can you all make out the stone and markings I am referring to?"

Angus's companions looked up and as they found the stone in question, agreed that it did indeed have some regular marking on its visible surface. They could not quite make out what the lettering said, if indeed it was lettering, and decided to call the curator for a ladder and a torch.

Only a few minutes passed before these two items arrived from the maintenance shed. Grant, being the youngest and most able, was elected to climb up and take a few photographs with Angus's digital camera.

"Can you make out the letters?" called Angus once Grant had reached the top of the ladder and maneuvered himself into position.

"The letters appear very similar to the markings on Tracy's token, just as you anticipated. Let me dust off the area and take some photographs. You will soon see for yourselves," replied Grant with a definite ring of excitement in his voice.

Grant took a number of photographs from different angles and before long descended with his findings. After everyone had viewed the images, they determined the markings on the stone were identical to those on Tracy's token, but it was still unclear what story the inscription told. However, Angus was now beaming with delight, which Elizabeth didn't fail to notice.

"Now Angus, I know you too well," Elizabeth teased. "From your look of satisfaction I would guess you are hiding something vital from us, something maybe only you with your vast experience of archaeology, ancient architecture, and relics would know about. What makes you feel so good?"

"Grant, did you notice any holes in the face of the stone, maybe a quarter inch in diameter but not very deep, only an inch or so?" asked Angus.

"I do believe there was at least one similar to what you describe," said Grant.

"Let me see the image on your camera again."

Grant examined the frontal image of the stone and confirmed there was a small hole as Angus had described. The cavity was situated in the center of the R that made up part of the anagram. It was easy to overlook, due to its placement within the lettering, a most effective form of concealment.

"Angus, I am sure you know the reason for this; please enlighten us. We have come too far now to play mind games. What's the purpose of this hole?" asked Grant with some frustration in his voice.

Angus examined a few other similar stones set into the wall at eye level, paying particular attention to the fit of the stones against each other.

"These are all weight-bearing stones, and any of them would be difficult to remove once the wall had been completed. I see from the photograph of the stone Grant inspected that the stone has signs of grouting or cementing around its edges. It is my belief that stone can be removed and reinserted at will.

"Let me further explain," continued Angus. "It was common during the Dark Ages and during times of religious and political persecution for the clergy to hide away their religious relics and documents in safe places. They frequently used false stones, and I believe this to be one of them. The safe hiding place was prepared by making a large cavity behind the stone, into which they deposited their treasures, or smaller cavities were hewn into the top surface of the stone for smaller artifacts. The problem once the objects had been hidden was how to recover them, how to extract such a fine fitting stone with no way to grip the edges, even after scraping away small quantities of grout. Many stones were not grouted, especially those situated indoors not exposed to the harsh weather. The hollow hole or cavity, such as we see in this stone disguised within the lettering, answered the problem."

Angus paused as once again all examined the photographs, which clearly showed the circular hole within the lettering. Now that they knew what to look for, the hidden hole became clear.

"So how does the hole help with extraction of the stone from the wall?" asked Tracy.

"The method is quite simple, even ingenious, but nothing new. I have seen the method used before during some of the archaeological digs I presided over in the Holy Land a number of years ago."

"Angus, stop procrastinating and get on with your explanation," exclaimed a now-impatient Elizabeth.

"All one needs to do is fit a soft wooden plug fully down into the bottom of the hole. Using a tool similar to an old-fashioned corkscrew but with a finer thread, screw the tool as far into the wooden plug as possible. The wooden plug will expand a little, and in so doing, tightly grips the interior surface of the hole and then, the stone can be extracted as far as required by pulling. The stone can also be reinserted and the plug removed by burning it out using a red hot poker. If required, the hole can be covered up with some grout, after which the position of the hole would be known to only a few," explained Angus.

"The fact this hole does not appear to have been covered indicates the stone has never been removed. It would therefore be reasonable to assume whatever was placed in or behind the stone is still there. Of course the prospect of finding nothing is likely; however, my instinct tells me otherwise."

A few minutes of lively discussion followed concerning this latest turn of events. Alan was the first to bring them back to the task at hand. "What do you propose we do now? Is there some protocol we must follow to examine the stone, and if so, can we proceed with the same level of confidentiality granted us so far?"

"I must first obtain permission from the director of Historic Scotland to extract the stone and also request him to ask the curator to continue helping us," replied Angus. "You have all come a long way. I sincerely hope we are now close to attaining our aspirations. We will surely know within the next few days."

Chapter 11

RING OF FAITH

Two full days passed before Angus and his friends reassembled at Rosslyn Chapel, having received permission to extract the marked stone only hours before. Angus had asked the university maintenance staff to fashion a corkscrew-like instrument to facilitate the stone being extracted from its present position. He had also prepared a number of soft conical larch wood plugs to be forced into the empty chamber. All was ready to start late afternoon when visitor hours ended.

Once again Grant, the youngest of the group, was elected to climb up to the stone. Having maneuvered himself into a stable position, he began by loosening the plaster sealant around the edges of the stone. He then inserted the wooden plug and attempted to use the screw in the fashion Angus had described two days earlier. It was not easy for those waiting impatiently below, especially Angus, who felt that all his efforts to this point would be for nothing if the marked stone did not give up any meaningful secrets. Even if it did, could those secrets be deciphered? Would they point to yet another secret rendezvous? And what if all their hopes were snuffed out, hopes built up as the years had passed by, hopes bolstered by recent events, but hopes Angus knew must end here if no significant information was revealed? The tension below became almost unbearable as Grant's progress seemed to come to a halt.

"Is the stone loosening at all?" inquired Angus, with more than a little anxiety in his voice.

"Yes! I think so," replied Grant. "Let me take out some more plasterwork; then I will attempt to move the stone a little to see if the sides are free. I think the weight of the stone will make it difficult to lift even the slightest amount."

Grant continued to work as more small pieces of debris and white dust fell to the chapel floor. After a few minutes Grant set down his tools, grasped the removal device, and pulled steadily while rocking the stone with small movements. The stone appeared to move a little with each pull. Time stood still for those waiting below. With every movement of the heavy stone, no matter how small, they waited with anticipation, hoping the stone would soon slide free.

"Be careful! As more of the stone comes out, the protruding part will not have any support," Angus called up anxiously.

"We may have to get something to support the weight, maybe a sort of trestle."

Angus had looked at other similar end stones and from their dimensions, estimated the stone Grant was working on to be about two feet in depth. He was going to stop extracting the stone when less than half was protruding unsupported, so as not to send it crashing down. A few more minutes passed. Little by little, more of the stone appeared. Angus was about to call a halt to the procedure when quite suddenly Grant exclaimed.

"I can feel a small cavity in the top of the stone! Another inch or so and it will be clearly in view. Do you think I should continue?" he inquired of Angus.

"Yes, continue," replied Angus. "Continue until you see how long and deep the cavity is. I think there is still plenty of well-supported stone to allow a few more inches of removal."

Grant continued. When the cavity was sufficiently clear for his hand to reach inside, he turned to those below, gave a wry smile and exclaimed, "Here we go, all or nothing. Any bets on what's inside?"

"Get on with it," they all cried back in unison.

Grant slid his now unsteady hand over the top of the stone and down into the small, uncovered cavity, fingers eagerly feeling ahead.

"What can you feel?" asked Tracy.

"There seems to be a small cloth bag—maybe muslin. I cannot quite get my fingers around it," replied Grant. "I'll need to ease the stone out a little more. Is that okay by you, Angus?"

"Yes, that will be fine," answered Angus.

Grant returned to the task at hand. He removed more small pieces of debris and inched the stone out a sufficient distance to reach down into the now-exposed cavity. A few seconds later, the muslin bag was in Grant's hands. He held the bag up for everyone to see and then descended slowly. Upon reaching the bottom rung of the ladder, he handed the bag to Angus.

Angus examined the bag carefully before cautiously loosening the drawstring and reaching inside. As everyone watched, barely daring to breathe, he retrieved a circular metallic object. Laying this token flat in the palm of his hand, he and his companions could see a similarity to the tokens each had already received; however, this token seemed larger in diameter and had raised, serrated sections around its circumference. The side with the serrated rim had some barely visible engraving; the reverse was polished, clear of any engraving, and flat without a rim. Everyone examined the token in turn, but nobody could explain the purpose of this new clue, and once again all looked to Angus for an explanation.

"It's a long time since I have seen anything like this," ventured Angus. "Do you have your token with you, Tracy?" he asked.

"Of course," replied Tracy. She dipped her hand deep into her purse and lifted out her token, now wrapped in soft tissue paper. She handed it over to Angus

Angus took her token. When he placed it over the token taken from the stone cavity, all could see that Tracy's token fitted precisely into the circular recess within the serrated edges. He pressed downward on Tracy's token and showed it could be rotated in either direction.

CAESARIAN DISK

Combination of Tracy's disk and ring from Rosslyn Chap

"Ladies and gentlemen, what we have here is an ancient form of a rotating cipher disk. When I say ancient form, I mean these discs have been around since Roman times; in fact, Julius Caesar developed a very elementary cipher, which seemed to serve him well, and because of who developed it, the process is called the Caesar Substitution cipher."

"Do you think a message to help us move on can be found by decoding the cipher you mention?" asked Tracy. She began playing with the two tokens, easily rotating them one inside the other in opposite directions

"Well, Tracy, I do hope so. However, it will not be easily done There are so many variables, so many combinations, but let me first explain," answered Angus, moving over to a small table and sitting down.

"Bring over those chairs and all of you sit down around the table; this explanation is going to take some time.

"Many historians believe the invention of writing was the true beginning of civilization," began Angus. "But not too long after writing became established, people found a need to communicate through writing that could only be read by the intended recipient. Some created codes, which use symbols or groups of letters to represent words or phrases. This invention, however, had one serious setback." Angus paused.

"So what was the setback?" asked Alan.

"Well, in the late nineteenth and early twentieth centuries, code books were created because telegram messages were charged by the word. Ten characters were considered a word by the telegraph companies and charged accordingly. Commercial code books were created about the same time other code books were used for security by both military and diplomatic organizations. However, there are disadvantages to code books. One is they are relatively bulky and thus more difficult to guard than, say, pocket-sized items. Another is they can be compromised if stolen, photographed, or otherwise copied. If replaced before anyone knew the book was missing, the thief would be able to decrypt any message without the owners' knowledge. Code books have since been made obsolete as ciphering technology has been developed. I believe what we have here to be one of the first pieces of cipher equipment ever created, and it was certainly used by monks as early as the fourteenth century." Angus looked around the table, expecting some questions.

"So are you saying Tracy's token, together with the token we have just found in the stone cavity, make up a form of cipher equipment?" inquired Grant.

"Yes, Tracy's token seems to be the inner ring, and the ring we have just found is the outer ring. But let me explain a little more," replied Angus.

The others waited enthralled with Angus's latest assertion. He certainly knew how to hold an audience.

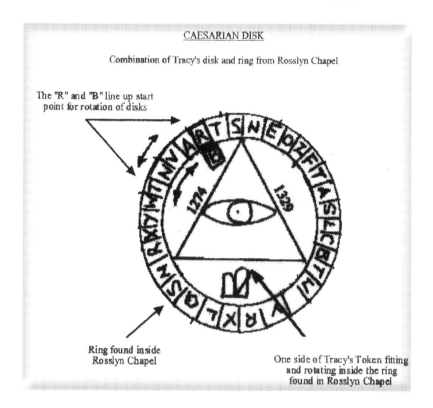

CAESARIAN DISK

Combination of Tracy's disk and ring from Rosslyn Chapel

The "R" and "B" line up start
point for rotation of disks

Ring found inside
Rosslyn Chapel

One side of Tracy's Token fitting
and rotating inside the ring
found in Rosslyn Chapel

"Cipher disks usually only employ alphabets or numbers, but occasionally the arrangement uses a combination of both alphabet *and* numbers. I believe the latter to be the arrangement we have before us. I think we can start the decoding process by aligning the letter R, which appears on the outer ring of the disk we found today, with the letter B on the inner ring that is engraved on the perimeter of Tracy's token. The letters R and B we agree refer to Robert Bruce. From this position, we can use the two dates on Tracy's token, the birth and death dates of King Robert, namely 1274 and 1329, when rotating the discs within each other. Rotating the discs will allow us to read off the ciphered message. The monks, or whoever left this ring in the stone cavity, intended to provide us with yet another clue to continue our quest.

"However," Angus added, raising the index finger of his right hand in emphasis, "there is one thing missing, one thing entirely impossible for us to solve quickly, and that is which direction to turn the disks, how far to turn each, and in what sequence. By that I mean, do we turn the digits of the birth date in one direction, let's say clockwise in sequence, then the death date digits in the opposite direction, counter-clockwise, or in any of the thousands of similar rotation combinations? We need the combination, just like we would need in order to open the simplest of office safe combination locks." Angus breathed out a heavy sigh of recognition, recognition of a seemingly insoluble dilemma.

"Well, I guess this is as far as I can go. I cannot remain in Scotland for much longer," said Grant.

"Me neither," echoed Tracy. "It seems to me Angus, Elizabeth, and Alan are the only persons having ample time to continue," she mused out aloud.

"Yes, it seems that way," replied Angus. "But there's always Sir Harold Spencer of Bletchley Park fame to help in this matter," he added with a twinkle in his eyes and a knowing grin spreading from cheek to cheek.

Chapter 12

COLOSSUS AND BERTHA

Not till the late 1980s did the existence of Britain's best kept secret of the Second World War become known to the general public. Bletchley Park had been on the classified information list for over forty years, having earned top secret classification.

Between 1939 and 1945, the most advanced and creative forms of mathematics and technological knowledge were combined to master German communications. Bletchley Park was the focus of all this research and knowledge. It would be no exaggeration to claim that British cryptanalysts, most notably Harold Spencer, changed the course of the Second World War, and coincidentally those working at Bletchley Park created the foundation of modem computers. Harold Spencer, now Sir Harold, having been knighted in the early 1960s, still lived near Bletchley Park. A few days after visiting Rosslyn Chapel, Angus and Elizabeth traveled south by train to Milton Keynes a few miles north of London to see Sir Harold, who still lived at Bletchley Park

Angus and Harold had served in the same intelligence regiment during the war. Although they kept in touch at Christmas and through regimental retired officers associations, they had never met these past fifty years, and so it was a very different-looking Harold that greeted Angus and Elizabeth at Milton Keynes railway station. The once ramrod-straight-backed young man with a mop of unruly red hair had aged dramatically. He was now some four inches shorter, his posture had taken on a pronounced stoop, the red hair of former times had become sparse and thin, and he walked with a shuffle. However, he certainly had a distinct twinkle in his eye, an infectious smile, and a most welcoming, although somewhat weak, handshake to greet Angus and the ever-present Elizabeth.

"Long time, no see," were Harold's first words of welcome.

"Aye, it's been too long," replied Angus before introducing Elizabeth. "I'm surprised you still live on the old premises, so to speak."

"Yes, I have been here almost all of my working and retired years," answered Harold.

"I presume after being here through the war and the many years up till your retirement must have made you feel so much a part of the place you could not drag yourself away. I remember Bletchley to be a charming house in a lovely location, and I well understand your reluctance to leave. I guess I may well have done the same thing if I had the opportunity. Ah! Such is life," replied Angus.

"Yes! I think you would have liked to have done the same. I remember how content you were here completing the projects we worked on together just after the war," said Harold. Then he continued, "A consortium led by Antony Slater—you may remember him from your days here—saved Bletchley Park from destruction in the early '90s and turned the property into a museum devoted to the recognition and reconstruction of the secret site. By doing so, he preserved for future generations a place that quite correctly could claim to have changed the course of history, and I was offered the position of custodian. I was also offered a piece of land close by but still on the premises, and it was there I built my small but comfortable home. As you know, I never married."

Their introductions over, Sir Harold suggested they go to his home to settle in. After unpacking, Angus and Elizabeth refreshed themselves after the long journey south from Edinburgh, changed clothes, and joined Harold in his sitting room. Small talk continued over a glass of sherry before they left to join a few of Harold's friends at a nearby pub for a modest evening meal. The conversation naturally turned to the happenings at Bletchley Park during Angus's service. Nothing was mentioned about the reasons for Angus's visit until after returning home, and it was after finishing his first of many cups of coffee that Harold asked, "Well, are you going to tell me about this conundrum you alluded to during our last conversation? I guess the solving of this mystery is your reason for traveling so far and at such short notice. From our conversation, I detected some urgency in your voice. What can I do for you?"

It took some time for Angus to share the story of his life's quest, but Harold listened intently, took down a few notes, and occasionally nodded approvingly. At last Angus came to speak about the cipher disk.

"Do you have the two tokens with you, the two you think when fitted together may make up an ancient cipher disk?" inquired Harold.

"Indeed I have," replied Angus.

He asked Elizabeth to pass him a small box he had given her for safekeeping just before leaving his Edinburgh office. Within the box, carefully wrapped between layers of soft tissue paper, lay the two tokens, one within the other. Angus unwrapped them, handed them to Harold, and waited with interest for Harold's comments. Naturally, he hoped they would be positive.

It took some time for Harold to fully examine the two tokens and think about Angus's assertions and hopes. After referring to one of many textbooks in his library, he returned to his place at the coffee table, and seemingly indifferent to the urgency of the situation, took some more time to gather his thoughts together.

"Certainly, as you say, Angus, these two tokens seem to make up an early form of what we know today as cipher disks, but they are not as simple as one would expect of disks made some seven hundred years ago. They not only have a combination of letters and numbers, but there are many other combinations available due to the rotation of the discs within each other. Even using the extremely powerful Colossus computer built in the early 1940s, we would find it exceedingly time consuming to program all the combinations possible to obtain some meaningful answers. What is missing? Some further step maybe. Another disk, perhaps, to fit over the two we have? I think not. This will be an extremely difficult entity to begin to decode even with the help of Colossus," concluded Harold, much to the frustration of Angus and Elizabeth.

"Are you telling us Colossus could, with time, break the code and give us alphabet equivalents to the numbers 1274 and 1329?" asked Angus.

"Yes," replied Harold. "But we would not know what those letters mean unless they were quite clear and explicit. I fear this would not be the case, and finding the meaning of the spelled out words—or maybe just plain letters of the alphabet—would prove to be a monumental task."

Angus and Elizabeth nodded in agreement.

"If I could get approval to run Colossus again, given a week or so I could reprogram the computer inputs and get a relevant printout of the most likely results. But then the only way for us to make a realistic, valid, and accurate assessment of the output would be to painstakingly compare our results to historic, geographic, and even linguistic data of the time when we thought the disk was encoded. Not impossible, but it would take weeks if not months of work, and I got the impression there was some urgency in your reasons for being here," said Harold, seemingly resting his case.

Angus and Elizabeth looked crestfallen at the apparent enormity of the task. Only a few minutes ago they seemed to have achieved a way to decode what they all now accepted to be two cipher disks, but their hopes had once again been dashed beyond repair. An awkward silence settled over the room. After a few minutes Harold rose from his chair, picked up a late edition of *Computer Science* magazine lying on his writing desk, and after opening it to a well-thumbed page, declared, "Maybe Jona Schultz can help!"

"Who is this Jona?" inquired Angus and Elizabeth in unison after a short silence.

Harold referred to the magazine again to get his facts correct and quoted from a bold-printed paragraph, 'British computer experts here at Bletchley recently acknowledged defeat by a German amateur radio enthusiast, one Jona Schultz, when he won a challenge to decode secret messages encoded by a World War II cipher machine. Jona, from Bonn, Germany, managed to intercept a special radio transmission and decipher a complex code in less than two hours. He used software he wrote for the challenge and finished the task while Britain's Colossus computer was still racing through its computations to come up with a solution. Schultz's computer program overcame the hardest part of the challenge, namely cracking the code sent by the SZ42 encrypting machine, which can generate approximately sixteen million, million permutations, and succeeded in doing so in just forty-six seconds!'

"Wow! That's some achievement," commented Angus, just beginning to imagine what Harold was about to suggest.

Harold then continued "It was a brilliant piece of work and really impressive. He used a program that was highly optimized for the task and was very well designed. However, pitting Colossus, which was designed in 1943 to '44, against modern computers may be considered unfair, but Jona is obviously brilliant at what he does, and I think it may be possible to get him interested in our problem. What do you think?" asked Harold.

"Well, sounds like a great idea to me," replied Angus.

Elizabeth nodded in agreement. "We certainly seem to have run out of any other viable options. How do you propose we get this Jona gentleman to help us? Are you well acquainted with him?"

Harold walked over to his oak writing desk, shuffled through some papers, and returned holding a letter bearing a German stamp.

"This is a personal letter I received from Jona only a few days ago. It's very strange how these things sometimes work out. Let me explain a little more, as I am sure you think this more than pure coincidence," said Harold. "As you may know, Angus, I was elected president of the Encryption Society two years ago. Earlier this year, I believe in late April, I and the whole board voted unanimously to offer Jona honorary life membership to the society in recognition of his brilliant work, and this letter here is his reply."

Harold unfolded the letter and quoted from it. "I am thrilled and delighted to be offered the honor of life membership. Please convey to the board I take great pleasure in accepting their kind and most appreciated offer. If there is anything I can do for the society, I would be available to do so at your pleasure."

Harold offered the letter to Angus to read through and then said, "This, Angus, may be the best bit of news we've heard in many a year. I think we should take him up on his offer. Maybe with his vast computer experience, he will take on the task of decoding. Just maybe he could give us the answer you need."

Angus raised an inquisitive eyebrow and looked across at Elizabeth. However, after shrugging and raising his hands in resignation to better judgment, he looked intently into Harold's eyes, saying, "I feel the best way to continue will be to follow your better-informed opinion in these matters. Can I leave our request for Jona's help to your own good self?"

"Well," said Harold, "we have known each other for many a year, and during that time I have been indebted to you on many occasions. This is what we can call payback time. Yes! Be well assured, I will try my best with Jona."

Angus and Elizabeth seemed to regain hope at this latest turn of events. Harold's promise, and his unsolicited help, was so much more than they had anticipated or even hoped for.

"Will you need to keep the two disks?" inquired Angus somewhat hesitantly.

"No, I think we can take digital photographs of both sides of the tokens and send them to Jona. If need be he could have a local craftsman replicate them. However, I think photographs will be quite sufficient for Jona to develop a computer program. I do know he loves challenges of this type."

A few days passed before Jona answered Harold's email describing the problem. Jona agreed that it was only necessary to send photographs at this stage. The photographs would allow him to assess the enormity of the problem, give the decoding method some serious thought, and advise Harold or Angus regarding his need, if any, for further information.

Later in the day, Harold took the clearest photographs showing all the markings on the two disks into his office and in a few minutes had the photographs scanned into his computer. An email to Jona was soon sent containing some further information and the photographs as attachments to the email. Harold then began an anxious wait for Jona's reply

Chapter 13

BERTHA'S RESPONSE

All through high school, Jona Schultz had been considered a computer geek. After high school he never outwardly showed interest in any other activities or indicated any meaningful relationship with anyone of the fairer sex. Nothing much in his character changed during his years at university or during his early adult life, but he had quite expectantly married Eva, a young lady from the outskirts of Bonn who shared the same nerdy interests, and now both were employed as research professors at Bonn University. They worked well together, contributing much to the world of computers, including advanced programming and research. Jona was highly regarded for his authorship of numerous publications and even more highly regarded for his much-publicized "defeat" of Colossus. Jona looked forward to his next challenge and perhaps another opportunity to enhance his reputation.

"Eva! Come through and look at the email I have just received from our dear friends at Bletchley," called Jona through his inter-office speaker system.

Eva occupied the office next to Jona's near the south end of the department of computer sciences. She gathered same papers together, pushed them to one side, and within a minute or so stood by her husband's side.

She examined the email and its attachments and said, "So this is from the Sir Harold Spencer you were telling me about last evening." She pondered a little and then continued, "These photographs would appear to be the subject of Sir Harold's request for your help in decoding the hidden messages. Do you have any thoughts yet, and would you like me to help, or do you wish to be your stubborn self and keep your work private?"

"Well, Eva, you were not involved with the beat-Colossus venture, so maybe it is time for us to work together on this new project. Harold said there are possibly ancient Scottish historical considerations. With your degree in medieval European history, you may certainly have knowledge way beyond mine in the historical field. I would very much welcome your advice and assistance, particularly with relevance to Scottish history once I start my computer programming on the subject.

"Harold said his friends in Scotland who gave him this project were running out of time to solve their conundrum. I suggest we set aside as much of our on-going work as we can and start on the decoding problem straight away. I will request Harold have his Scottish friends forward as much information and ideas they have regarding avenues of investigation, historical time periods, languages, ciphers, and the like directly to me. I will advise the dean we need a short vacation; the department certainly owes us vacation time considering the many extra hours we have been working of late."

During the next few days Jona exchanged a number of telephone calls with Angus, who had returned to his Edinburgh office. He gathered as much of the information about the tokens as he could through further emails, and he also sent Jona copies of the Euboean Alphabet Ian McDougall had used to decipher the words "Brus Mask."

Once Jona assured himself Angus had forwarded all information of consequence, he and Eva set aside their assignments and began working exclusively on solving what Jona now called "Project Destiny."

"The program I used to defeat Colossus is of little use in solving Project Destiny," confided Jona to Eva after a few days' work. He then added deliberately and thoughtfully, "The parameters are almost three dimensional when one includes historical nuances and the possibility of answers in French, Old English, and the many dialects of Scots English used during the thirteenth century. The core difficulty appears to be the Caesarean cipher problem. Unless we solve that first, we will be very much in the dark and without a way to decipher the rest of the problem. The number of solutions given by rotating the discs within one another, in both direction and distance, are almost immeasurable. Even though we achieve what appears to be a valid answer, we could very well run into another problem, namely selecting an answer generated by Bertha that best suits Angus's needs. It may be possible we mistakenly give Angus an answer that appears feasible to us but is in fact well out of context in time and location regarding Angus's search."

"Do you think Bertha will be up to the task once you have prepared a specialized program?" inquired Eva, referring to Jona's high-speed computer. "There is little for me to work on until we get a language printout from Bertha. Only then could I hope to put the words into context and help Angus find where the stone has lain hidden these many centuries."

"Yes, Eva, that very well may be the case. I will complete my programming tonight, run Bertha in the morning, and see what, if anything, comes to light."

Over the next two days, Jona and Eva adjusted their programming after completion of every two-hour run ended. Each run provided inconclusive, although consistent, results. Even though Bertha was generating more than twenty billion permutations every hour, both Jona and Eva became increasingly disappointed at their lack of seemingly valid conclusions.

"There has to be something missing, something relating to the way the cipher discs rotate within one another. There must be a key that explains in which direction and how far to rotate the discs. We are now using Bertha to bypass that step and produce an answer that should be much easier to come by. After all, fourteenth-century communications involved little more than the cleft stick or the carrier pigeon. It is entirely possible a very simple code is looking Angus and his cohorts in the face! We can only accept and report the results of five computer runs, no matter how irrational they appear to us here in Bonn. What do you think, Eva?" asked Jona.

"I agree," replied Eva. "We do not have enough numeric or algebraic information for us to realistically investigate further. I feel you have done your best, probably the best anyone in our field can do, and I cannot in good faith say I can add anything of value. Let us send our results as they are, leave the printout in English, and maybe someone Angus knows with a good working knowledge of the Scots dialect will see a connection through a place, name, or significant event."

Knowing time was of the essence, Jona telephoned Angus advising him of the decision he and Eva had reached. He apologized for not having achieved any obvious solution to the challenge Angus had posed. Jona did not take kindly to defeat. He admitted to Angus that the five different Bertha runs provided very similar printouts that could very well be of great value, but not in a way that was obvious to him.

It took two days before a courier service managed to get Angus's signature for the delivery of Jona's letter. The outwardly insignificant envelope containing a summary of the printouts quivered in Angus's eager hands as he called for Elizabeth to join him in his office. He instinctively knew he was about to read some response that would lead the token holders or Elizabeth to the answer. Surely his life's quest would not end here now. It would not end with negative words from Jona, someone he had relied upon to unlock the secrets of the cipher discs. Angus slowly opened the envelope, removed the single sheet of paper, and slowly read the contents out loud to Elizabeth, who was now standing nervously by his right side.

Dear Professor Gillespie,

I was greatly honored to work with you in trying to solve what I have called Project Destiny. Regrettably, although my wife, Eva, and I devoted a number of days to reprogramming my computer Bertha, the same computer I used during the Colossus-breaking competition, I feel we have not had any conclusive results.

I will not go into the various reasons, but suffice it to say this was not entirely a mathematical conundrum. There are too many outside variables, such as language and historical data, which preclude the achievement of what I feel would be a meaningful valid conclusion to the computer runs we carried out these past few days. But not all is bad and inconclusive.

We carried out five exhaustive computer runs, each with different input programs. Fortunately, three of the runs did produce similar results. These results, although not making any sense to us here in Bonn, may be of value to you and your staff. Hopefully somebody will recognize the following words and deduce a meaning.

When we used only the numbers you sent, 1274 and 1329, as computer inputs, three of computer runs resulted in two four-letter word print-outs. Those numbers were the numbers, or as you suggested historical dates, taken from the center rotating token making up one of the Caesarean cipher discs.

These two print-out words are "anet" and "fall," and I have presumed these two words to be English although we cannot find "anet" in any English dictionary. Of course, anet may have meaning in the ancient Scots language or one of the language dialects, and we will leave it to your local resources to hopefully determine that meaning.

Both Eva and I very much hope we have given you something to work on. We both wish you all the very best with your continuing search.

Best regards,

Jona

Angus and Elizabeth seemed somewhat dejected at Jona's news. They read the letter over a few times, hoping to read something more positive and encouraging between the lines. Soon, however, they came to accept the contents of Jona's letter.

"What now?" queried Elizabeth. "There does not seem to be much sense to be made of the two words Jona's computer has supplied. What do you think, Angus? You seem deep in thought these past ten minutes or so."

Angus did not reply but crossed over to his book cabinet, took down a copy of the *Oxford Concise English Dictionary* and started thumbing through it. He stopped at the letter F.

"Let's start with looking up the word fall," said Angus. "We have a variety of meanings, so let's begin by going through them in order. Look, there appears to be many uses of the word, including the use of the word as meaning 'autumn' in the United States. That leaves a lot to choose from, but I am sure we can eliminate most of them as being the wrong sense for the context. Would you not think so?"

"Yes," replied Elizabeth. "But what about the other word anet? Do you think that could be a place name or adjective describing someplace? I must admit although the word does seem somewhat familiar; I just cannot place where I remember it from."

"Let's leave that for now and concentrate on the dictionary meaning of fall," interrupted Angus. "You read through the dictionary and come up with about five or six definitions you prefer and feel are relevant. I will go and advise our token holders of this latest progress and ask them to meet with us here as quickly as possible."

Angus sent out the necessary emails to Alan, Grant, and Tracy advising them of the content of Jona's letter. He asked when each would be available to meet with him and Elizabeth in his office, preferably as soon as possible. He knew Tracy had returned to her position in Qatar but hoped both Alan and Grant, Alan living less than an hour away and Grant still on vacation, would be able to meet quickly. Angus was not disappointed. Within hours both Alan and Grant had responded and confirmed they were able to meet any time the next day. Angus cancelled a couple of appointments and prepared to meet both Alan and Grant at 2:00 the next afternoon.

Angus referenced another dictionary from before 1900 in the university main library while Elizabeth scrutinized his more modern office copy. He felt some different meanings of the word fall may have been in use more than a hundred years ago. Those meanings may have been omitted from the concise Oxford edition, and he wished to cover that eventuality. He scribbled down a number of meanings and related entries and returned to his office.

"So what have you got for me?" Angus asked Elizabeth after she had looked through all the dictionary definitions of fall and associated terms she deemed relevant.

"There are a few definitions, four to be precise, I think are worth looking into," replied Elizabeth. "I have written them down. Let's hope the definitions you selected from the older dictionary will match some of mine. That at least would be some progress."

Angus laid out his selections and they compared notes.

"I see we have picked two similar definitions from our selections. The two we have selected are not precise definitions of fall but associated words. You have selected 'a downward slope, or declivity' and 'a cataract, or waterfall,' and I have also selected two similar meanings from my older dictionary. There are a number of other meanings, but these both seem to refer to a place or place name. Let's keep these in mind for now until we meet with the others. Continue to think about the other word, anet. Maybe something in the depths of our memories will spring to mind."

Alan and Grant arrived at Angus's office a little before 2:00 the next afternoon. Both clearly appeared keen to hear Angus's judgment, an explanation of Jona's letter, and the implications of his findings. A few minutes earlier an email had arrived from Tracy in which she expressed her sincere regrets at not being able to attend their meeting. She asked to be kept updated on the latest developments, wished them all great success, and hoped she would be able to travel to Edinburgh at short notice if needed in the near future. Angus read her letter to all present.

It took Angus a few minutes to inform Alan and Grant of the contents of Jona's letter and to give them his opinion about the two key words and the definitions he and Elizabeth had concluded were most relevant. Silence fell over the office as each pondered Jona's findings and searched their memories for other explanations or hidden meanings; none came to mind. Alan then thought aloud.

"It seems to me we must conclude the monks of Scone Abbey would have tried to indicate the place where they hid the stone, someplace secure yet easily accessible. Someplace able to endure the passage of time and easily identified by two words; hopefully the words contained in Jona's letter. I like the meaning 'cataract, or waterfall.' But which word and where?"

"How about Anet Waterfall?" asked Elizabeth. Then she continued, "Is there such a place? Did such a name even exist long ago? Sounds like another gigantic search to me, like trying to find the pot of gold at the end of a rainbow!"

She sat down, visibly frustrated and near the end of her patience with the whole experience.

"Elizabeth, I got the impression from Angus that you had said you were familiar with the word anet. Is that correct?" asked Alan. "Well, initially I too had a fleeting response in my mind, but, like you, I just cannot place where I know it from, if indeed I do. Maybe it had something to do with a bank location that had something to do with my banking career. Who knows? Just another frustrating thought!"

Further thoughts, ideas, and even dreams were discussed, but all to no avail. Eventually Angus decided to bring the meeting to a halt, but first he asked if he could advise Tracy of their impasse and see if she could add anything of value.

"I don't see why not," replied Grant. After all, anything would be better than nothing. Let's hope she will have something meaningful to add."

Alan and Grant left the office together, each agreeing to search their memories deeply over the next few days, but each also knowing the sheer size of the task that lay ahead. Angus poured himself and Elizabeth a large whisky to cap what had proved to be an eventful but quite frustrating afternoon's work.

"Let us hope a good night's sleep will stimulate our memories and enlighten us," said Angus, locking his office door as he and Elizabeth started for home.

Chapter 14

REVEALED MEMORIES

A short email arrived from Tracy. She expressed her frustration at not being able to shed any light upon the problem but interestingly, added she too had some recollection of the word anet or a similar word. Once again she too could not recall the circumstances.

"Well, that's three people who seemingly have some recollection of the word, you, Elizabeth, Alan, and Tracy," said Angus as he relayed the contents of Tracy's email.

"Yes," replied Elizabeth. "We must think of something we all have in common, an experience we three have had, a book we have all read, a place we've visited, just something to connect us in a way we appear to be overlooking."

Angus agreed with Elizabeth's remarks and then added, "I recall both Tracy and Alan saying they had visited Scone Palace, which is near the old Scone Abbey. Tracy visited when she was a young girl during a daytrip from school, and Alan later in life after his retirement to Blair. When was it you visited, Elizabeth?"

"Oh, I went just after the Queen's coronation in 1953, part of a group of recent graduates from university. I was so interested hearing the history of our ancient kings being crowned nearby, seeing Boot Hill, where their coronations took place, and listening to all the folklore and legends concerning those times. I remember our guide, a relatively young lady not much older than any of us, as having quite an extraordinary ability to make our tour come to life."

"Can you recall any of her stories?" asked Angus. "Do you remember any reference to the stone?"

Angus paused a few seconds and then continued, "Your visit was shortly after four Scottish students had removed the stone from under the present-day coronation chair in Westminster Abbey. Maybe Tracy heard the same talk from the same guide when she visited with her school friends. Her visit would most likely have been around the same time, although she would have been much younger."

The next day Angus phoned Alan and asked when he first visited Scone Palace, hoping he had been there around the same time as Tracy and Elizabeth, but regrettably that proved not to be the case. Alan replied he had visited only ten or so years ago with other members of the Blair Historical Society. They did not have the services of a guide, but he did bring back a number of brochures and pamphlets. He said he had stored them away to help him give some short lectures concerning the palace and its surrounds to members of the society.

Alan finished the conversation by saying, "I do remember purchasing a small booklet relating the history of the long-time owners of Scone Palace, the Earl of Mansfield's family, and notable events during the family's ownership. I do remember finding that booklet fascinating reading, although I read it some time ago now. I will try and find it, read it through again, and let you know if I read anything of interest regarding the stone. I'm pretty sure there were some references to it, but then maybe not; it's been so long."

"Yes, please do," replied Angus. "I feel Tracy, Elizabeth, and now you have some deep memories regarding the word anet. I sense that sooner or later one of you will drag up some memory of the word from your subconscious. You just need a trigger, and that can come at anytime from anywhere. Hopefully it will come sooner than later. I just hope we do not run out of time. After all, there's only a few months left before the coronation."

Alan searched through all his correspondence, references, and articles of historical interest that evening along with Adith, his lovely Chinese significant other and current golfing competition partner. Adith came upon a booklet titled *The Earls of Mansfield Chronicles*. She found the almost-new booklet in one of Alan's older filing cabinets.

"Is this what you are looking for, Alan?" inquired Adith, passing to him the booklet. "It has the word *Mansfield* in the title. Maybe our bad luck has changed!"

"Great job, Adith," replied Alan, taking the booklet from her outstretched hand and immediately thumbing through the hundred or so pages.

That evening Alan started to read through the Mansfield story, which contained much of interest, particularly references to the many myths and legends handed down through the three hundred years of Mansfield ownership of the palace and the surrounding lands. However, nothing seemed to trigger his memory. Somewhat disappointed, he and Adith retired to bed just after midnight, but he hardly slept. His mind turned over and over; the answer seemed to be on the tip of his tongue. Maybe the following day with new pages to be read and minutely examined, would get some response from his blank and now-weary memory.

Breakfast came and went; page after page was scrutinized for even the smallest of clues, but to no avail. Then, halfway down page eighty-three, Alan suddenly saw the words that sparked his memory.

"Quick, Adith, come here!" he shouted into the living room, where Adith was reading the morning paper. "See what I have found! Look at these words, words locked up in my memory until now—words which I believe will provide us with answers."

Adith read a paragraph relating a most relevant legend Alan had underlined in pencil: "On the approach of King Edward's army, the monks hurriedly removed the Stone of Destiny to a place of safe concealment, and replaced it with a stone of similar size and shape taken from the Anetty burn which the king carried off in triumph."

Alan, almost unable to contain himself, explained. "You see the words 'Anetty burn'? The word 'burn' means 'small stream' in Scots dialect. These words indicate there existed a stream of that name in those days, and that stream must be named after a place or source not far from Scone. We must search for that stream; search for a place name, a village present or past, a farm, indeed any area of land or water including that name."

"Indeed we must," agreed Adith. "I am sure Angus and the others will be delighted to hear about you finding this connection."

On hearing Alan's news, Angus was delighted. Elizabeth too remembered the word Anetty; she recalled it being used by the Scone Palace guide during her talk about the palace's history. She now remembered the guide had related a legend dating from about the same time that told of two young farm workers entering a fissure scoured deep into a local hillside. This fissure had been caused by a landslide, and once well inside, the workers came across what appeared to be some ancient artifacts. Many years later, one of the workers heard stories concerning the whereabouts of the stone and searched the area but could not find the fissure. Most people hearing this yarn considered the account to be just an exaggerated, if not entirely imagined, tale.

"I wonder if this legend is true, and if so, whether the circumstances would be of great significance. That really would be more than we could ever hope for," said Elizabeth.

"Truth is often much stranger than fiction," commented Angus. "But we have much work to do, much more searching to do, and I know just where to go."

"And where may that be?" questioned Elizabeth.

"The Signet Library, where many of Scotland's ancient documents are to be found," answered the alert and interested Angus.

He seated himself, looked Elizabeth squarely in the eyes, and declared, "I feel our search will soon be over. I feel this latest clue may just fit and open the lock."

Chapter 15

ANCIENT MAPS AND A
WELCOME SIGN

The Signet Library lay within the old Scottish Parliament House building complex. These ancient buildings were situated on the south side of the High Street, which connected Edinburgh Castle and its esplanade to Holyrood Palace. Edinburgh City Hall and the Lord Provost's offices were almost directly opposite the library in the area commonly called the Old Town of Edinburgh. The library was also close to Angus's university office. Although the library was mostly used by lawyers associated with cases in the High Court, also situated in Parliament House, some university professors had access to the library and its vast store of ancient documents and maps. Angus was one of those afforded this privilege. He had used the library frequently in association with his archaeological projects, knew the staff well, and could count on the librarian to locate any documents, especially those dating earlier than the eighteenth century. Also located on the south side were the Old Scottish Parliament chambers. Here, priceless paintings and sculptures lined the oak walls that supported one of Scotland's most famous exquisitely designed and carved wood-beamed ceilings. Here lawyers and their clients observed the old tradition of discussing their cases while pacing the echoing wood floor. This old practice ensured any would-be eavesdropper would only snatch an occasional phase, thus ensuring complete lawyer-client privacy.

"Good morning, Angus. I did receive your message requesting my help," said Andy, the long-time librarian. "Not seen you in quite a while. What can I do for you and the lovely Elizabeth? It must be of some importance, as my secretary says you certainly seemed anxious to use the library as soon as possible."

"Andy, please trust me on this one. I cannot tell you why, but I must with some urgency examine all of your seventeenth—and eighteenth-century maps of central Perthshire, particularly estate maps, showing areas within a fifty-mile range of Scone Palace and Scone Abbey. Do you have any I can view today?" asked Angus, keen to start his search.

"Well, you never fail to surprise me," replied Andy. "Let me look in our computerized inventory, see what we have that fits your request, and see if I can get them to you within the next hour or two. I do hope we have better luck than the last time, when I believe you were looking for some letters written by our long-departed Queen Victoria to her manservant John Brown."

"Yes, you remember correctly," replied Angus. "Elizabeth and I will have an early pub lunch across the road, probably in the Volunteer, and meet you back here at one o'clock."

The Volunteer dated back to the early eighteenth century. Many would-be poets and writers hoping to emulate Sir Walter Scott or Robert Burns had sought inspiration, good food, and ale there, just as their more-famous predecessors had done more than two hundred years earlier. Dark wooden panels lined the engraved-glass-decorated walls. Similarly ornate shoulder-high wood dividers separated four—and six-seat booths, each with a glass-topped wood table where patrons sat discussing events of the day. Pies and sandwiches seemed to be a favorite choice for lunch, all washed down with a pint or two of good locally brewed Scottish ale. Elizabeth chose a small pork pie with cheese and onion slices on the side; Angus, his favorite locally made lamb haggis and mashed potatoes. Both drank a small lager.

After lunch, as Angus and Elizabeth walked back across the cobbled courtyard in front of Parliament House, they heard the one o'clock gun fire high up on the castle ramparts.

"We are in good time," declared Angus. "The gun is always on time. It must have been the Edinburgh timepiece for over one hundred fifty years now, and many think the gun firing is a much appreciated, traditional event."

Andy was waiting by the entrance at the library security desk. He signed Angus and Elizabeth in, listing them as present for research purposes, and took them down to the lower chambers. There he pointed at a number of files and three leather-bound books lying on one of the large time-aged oak tables standing alone within viewing cubicles. They noticed the absence of chairs and the presence of an elderly, but alert, member of the security staff whom Angus presumed was there to prevent any photography or tampering with the artifacts.

"The maps you asked for are all inside these leather bindings and date from the era you requested. They have been sent over to me by the curator of the Map Library of Scotland in Salisbury Place a few minutes' walk away. Look at them this one time, take notes at will, but please keep your time here as short as possible. We have to secure this lower chamber while you are here. We close at four, which gives you just under three hours to complete your research. Do let the attendant know when you are finished, and he will escort you to my office just inside the first level entrance after signing you both out." Andy smiled, shook Elizabeth's and Angus's hands, and wished them good luck before returning to the upper chambers.

"I think it best to start with a thorough search through each of the maps," declared Angus, automatically taking charge just as if he were at one of his archaeological digs. "Both of us should search at the same time on the same map so that we back each other up. We will be able to confirm and validate any relevant findings, and one of us should take notes of all we do as we search each page of each book. We must not miss anything now that we have come this far."

"Before we start, tell me exactly what we are we looking for," queried Elizabeth. "Are we searching for a village or tower name, or even the name of a dried-up river? You have not made that clear to me yet. I think our search must be more specific."

"Well, let's start looking for any inscription with the word anet standing by itself as a noun or adjective," replied Angus.

They opened the first folder of maps.

It took more than two hours to go through the first two books. The maps had been drawn near the turn of the eighteenth century, and although both Angus and Elizabeth found many places of interest that still appeared on modern-day atlases, nothing seemed to relate at all to the words they sought.

"I fear I'm getting tired and sore scanning these twenty or so maps. Bending over like this certainly proves the library staff does not want anyone spending hours down here," commented Elizabeth as she stood up, stretched her aching back, and leaned against the oak table.

"I too have a fear," replied Angus. "Not a physical one like you, but the fear of failing again. After all, we have now searched through two books without even the smallest success and have just one book more to study. If we are unsuccessful all our hopes will have to be directed elsewhere."

Elizabeth agreed, pulled the remaining book over between them, and opened it to the first page of what appeared to be a book of estate maps. This book consisted of only a few pages, no more than five. All of the pages were discolored a dull brown, and although they seemed in good condition, they appeared quite fragile and were cracked and slightly torn around their edges. No dates or similar annotations appeared on the book's cover or on any of the lightly bound maps.

"This will not take long," Elizabeth thought out loud.

Angus, almost resigning himself to yet another disappointment, another false although initially credible lead, agreed.

Yet, on second glance, this third book appeared to be quite different from the two they had previously examined. The cartography, boundary lines, and names of places were drawn much more finely and delicately. The coloring was dull, and the coats of arms depicted in the corners of each page were considerably faded. This map was obviously much older than the others. Angus recognized the handwritten notations besides some features were in French. Rough sketches of towers, spires, and battlements were evident, although some were hardly discernable, as if deliberately erased.

Angus's spirits rose dramatically. He stood back from the table, hands on hips, and said, "Elizabeth, the answer lies somewhere within in these pages. We are looking at a much older map, maybe from the late fourteenth century. Experience tells me these pages were produced by one of the few artists around in those days, maybe someone from a priory or monastery, perhaps someone who illustrated Holy Scriptures. The most significant fact about these hand-scribed maps is that the only priory in these parts recorded to be active in these times was the priory at Scone Abbey. These maps, in my opinion, were drawn by a monk or monks living during the time when the stone was taken from the abbey to London by Edward's army. There must be an answer in these pages."

With renewed energy, Elizabeth and Angus continued closely examining each page until Angus tapped Elizabeth on the arm and exclaimed, "What was that other legend you remember hearing? Something about soldiers carrying branches of trees before them to disguise them as a marching forest? Certainly it was something like that?"

"Oh, that was the story about Dunsinane Hill. I guess the same hill mentioned in Shakespeare's *Macbeth*," said Elizabeth. "A lookout in his castle at Dunsinane Hill reported Birnam Wood marching south, as prophesied by the three witches and indicating Macbeth's eventual demise at the hands of Malcolm Canmore, who eventually took his crown."

"Yes, I remember now," replied Angus.

"Look for Dunsinane, or a placename something like that, it cannot be too far from Scone. The Earl of Mansfield's property extends twenty miles from the palace where he still resides."

"Look here, Angus," exclaimed Elizabeth. "Look at this hill with symbols indicting battlement remains around one side just fifteen miles due east of the old abbey. There are some letters hardly discernable to the naked eye marking the spot. What do you think?"

Angus leaned over, and using one of the library's magnifying glasses, agreed there was indeed some form of battlement. A barely discernable inscription was drawn around what appeared to be contour lines that defined a hill of some magnitude. However, much to Angus's delight, he could make out the letters "nsin," presumably the middle letters of Dunsinane. The rest of the word must have been erased by time, he concluded.

"And not only that, my dear," whispered Angus. "Just look below the middle letters, where a stream runs east to west and where a sketch of some settlement appears. Do you see the words 'Village of Anet'? I cannot quite make out all the letters, but I can certainly see three, and the last word definitely ends with the letters 'net.'"

Elizabeth, now knowing where and what to look for, confirmed Angus's find. They both looked with smiling affection upon each other, embraced, and shook hands, much to the surprise of the attendant, and quietly whispered words of congratulations.

"What now?" whispered Elizabeth, hardly controlling her pent-up emotions.

"We must copy this parchment drawing by hand, purchase a modern-day survey map of this area, and advise Alan of these latest encouraging developments. After all, he lives only a few miles north, in Blair. I should think no longer than a twenty-minute drive to Dunsinane Hill."

Angus related the good news to Alan and arranged for both he and Elizabeth to meet Alan at the entrance to the Scone Palace car park two days later. Alan was familiar with the location of Dunsinane Hill. He had never visited the ancient ruins near the hill's summit, although he was well acquainted with the life of Macbeth and his eventual demise. He was most interested in seeing the drawing Elizabeth had made of the area and thought it would only be some twenty or so minutes to drive to the village of Collace, where his local maps showed a hiking trail leading up to the battlement ruins of Macbeth's castle. These he believed were the very same battlements shown on the parchment.

They departed the palace car park shortly after noon, and taking the main Scone road to Cupar, Angus soon reached the Collace signpost and followed two miles of narrow, winding roads to the village. They parked on a small grassy area near a clearly well-used footpath leading off to the south and up to a hill marked on their map as Kings Seat.

"I think we should start up this path," suggested Alan. "You can see from the map a small stream crosses the path some way up at a point called Macbeth's well. Another nameless stream east of the well runs north. Let's make for that point."

"Sounds like a plan to me," replied Angus as they started up the footpath.

After a few minutes into the climb, Angus noticed a rough farmyard track leading off to the left. This track was not on his map, and he wondered why.

"This track seems to lead in the direction of the ruins of the village marked as Anet on the old map. Although I do not see any ruins, I'm sure they must be above the farmyard," he exclaimed. "I do not think we need to go higher, but I suggest we follow this track further to the east. It seems to lead to that farm with the red-roofed barn and some agricultural equipment parked nearby. The stream we saw earlier on the old map seems to be beyond the farmyard, probably in the gully higher up, where those tall fir trees stand."

All agreed to Angus's suggestion and started off toward the farmhouse. Within a few minutes, they came to a weather-worn sign that read, "ANETTY FARM. PRIVATE. DO NOT TRESPASS."

Alan, Elizabeth, and Angus gazed at the sign in stunned silence. The farm sign seemed almost too good to be true. Was the stream running through the small valley to the west of the farm really the Anetty burn? Were they now much closer to the actual hiding place of the real Stone of Destiny?

"I think we must approach the farm owner before proceeding further," stated Angus. "Although there are not supposed to be any trespassing laws in Scotland, it would only be good manners to ask the farmer for permission to proceed across his land before climbing up to the stream's source. He may answer questions we have and tell us even more about the local area and its history."

Angus pressed the farmhouse doorbell and waited. No one came to the door. Two more presses of the bell had no effect, but after three sharp raps on the door, someone could be heard moving inside. Soon the door opened.

"Kin ah help you in any way?" inquired a rather stout middle-aged man with thinning grey hair, a weather-beaten complexion, and piercing blue eyes.

"We were hoping to speak with the farm owner concerning some archaeological and geological investigations we would like to carry out. We would like permission to cross the farm property and proceed up the burn to its source and look at the rock formations and structure in the vicinity of any waterfall," said Angus. He stepped back a little from the doorstep and offered the man his university identification card and his personal driving license.

"Aye, my name's MacFarlane and I've been farming hereabouts for many a year. Aye, you're speaking to the right man," replied the farmer in his thick Perthshire accent.

"I can tell you it's a tough climb up above the tree-line. There's an old right-of-way path you can all follow, but it's very muddy after all the rain we had this week. However, you are all welcome to go up as far as you can get hiking over the farm property. My youngest son is going to Edinburgh University, so anything I can do to help the staff would be my pleasure."

Angus extended his hand in thanks and then asked, "Is there a waterfall of any size farther up above the tree-line?"

"Aye there is," replied the farmer. "There's not much water in it at the back end of summer, but when the loch above the fall fills up after the spring snow melt, there's a spate that makes the pool below almost overflow. Its then the local children can catch some good-size trout."

Angus, Alan, and Elizabeth said their many thanks, took their leave of farmer MacFarlane, and made off to the path leading uphill beside the Anetty burn.

MacFarlane proved to be correct about the path's condition. Stretches of deep mud lay in ruts created by hundreds of sheep hoofs during the animals' trip to the burn for water. After some thirty minutes' difficult climb, Angus, Alan, and Elizabeth arrived at an open space just above the tree-line beside the pool MacFarlane had described. Descending to the pool, they found a waterfall about twenty feet high but with little water falling. A few trout flashed out of sight under an overhanging rock just below the pool's surface.

Either side of the fall was a mass of spiky gorse, green, and brown ferns, and overhanging boughs from a cluster of birch trees. Green and yellow mosses and fungi clung to the rock face. All appreciated this idyllic scene as they sat to rest on a large rock where the water overflowed out of the pool.

"Angus, do you have my drawing of the parchment map with you?" inquired Elizabeth. "I need to look at it again to confirm my thoughts about the position of some features."

Angus fumbled inside his jacket and handed over the crumpled map. Elizabeth studied the map for some time and then asked, "Did MacFarlane say there was a loch above the falls that filled up in winter and increased the water flow significantly?"

"Yes," replied Angus. "Why do you ask?"

Elizabeth held out the map to Angus and Alan and added, "I cannot see any sign of a loch or any other place that could hold water above the falls. Why do you think it is not shown?"

"Well, maybe it was not there then," replied Alan.

"Yes, that's a good point," said Angus. "So how and when was it formed? I think we should climb up above the falls and see for ourselves."

After a few minutes clambering up the more easily accessible west side of the falls, they arrived at a grassy knoll where the still waters of quite a sizable loch lapped. The peat-stained waters stretched back at least a mile or so; the breadth appeared to be at least three hundred yards.

"Certainly a loch this size would surely appear on any maps of the area such as those we examined in the Signet Library," commented Angus. "Unless, of course, the loch formed after the map was drawn. Looking up the hill there to the left, I believe that was exactly the case."

Elizabeth, Alan, and Angus looked up in the direction Angus pointed.

"You can quite clearly see from that wide gully that there has been a landslide. A landslide of some magnitude would have blocked the burn above the falls and caused the loch to form."

"I see," said Elizabeth. "The legend of the farmhands finding a crevice in the hillside after a storm and entering to find some ancient stone artifacts could very well be true. The crevice was not formed by the storm; it had been here all the time behind the waterfall. When the water stopped flowing due to the landslide, the crevice became visible. After the loch filled up with water, which could have taken months or even years, the water flowed again along its original course, so the crevice would no longer have been visible."

"Yes, Elizabeth, quite so," replied Angus with a contented tone of voice. "I believe we are nearing the end of our search. What are your thoughts, Alan?"

Alan, a little more cautious, replied, "I think we must either block the water flow again or get very wet entering through the waterfall to get into any crevice behind it, if indeed there is one. I personally think all signs now point to there being some kind of cave behind the waterfall. We will only know by exploring further. I do not think it feasible to stop the waterfall, so we must try to get behind the water, and soon, before the flow gets too great, which will happen once the wet weather arrives."

Angus and Elizabeth both nodded in agreement. After a short discussion, all agreed nothing more could be achieved without proper caving equipment, waterproof gear, and some form of lighting and communication devices. All three started the much easier descent to MacFarlane's farmhouse. Soon Angus was knocking on the wood-paneled front door, hoping MacFarlane was still at home, although it had been more than two hours since their first meeting.

"Aye, I see from your muddied feet you must have made it up to the fall," said MacFarlane as he answered the door. "It's a fairly tough climb especially for you, my dearie." Then, still looking at Elizabeth, he continued, "Did you find what you were looking for?"

Angus replied that they had some success, but they needed to return at least one more time with a bigger party and some scientific and digging equipment to complete their investigation.

"I don't see any problem with that," replied the farmer. "Just give me a wee warning about what day and time you'll be here, and all should be fine."

Angus once again proffered his sincere thanks to MacFarlane and said they would be back in a couple of days, but not before calling well ahead of time. Angus, Elizabeth, and Alan then made their way back to the car.

Two days passed before Angus and his party, now five people, presented themselves at farmer MacFarlane's house again. This time, the farmer was attending to chores inside the cattle byre, and upon seeing Angus's party approach the farmhouse, he walked over to greet them.

"Aye, you've picked a good day to go back up the hill," he said, referring to the good weather. "I just hope this time you find what you're all looking for." With a good-natured wave of his hand, he directed them to the burn-side path.

Grant had met the party at Scone Palace car park. Once there he was soon joined with Angus, Alan, Elizabeth, and James Armstrong, a young Scots archaeologist among Angus's most-trusted staff. Ian had often helped Angus in his search for the stone.

The mud had almost completely dried, and the party made good time climbing up to the waterfall. Upon arriving, they unpacked their caving tackle and the other equipment Angus had deemed necessary to help progress. Included in the extra search tackle were two fully oiled hurricane lamps, a selection of large and small flashlights, and a coil of thin white nylon cord at least three hundred feet long. Two walkie-talkies, with spare batteries, and two boxes of matches completed the necessary extra equipment. Alan produced three sets of waterproof clothing, similar to that worn by fishermen, and three waterproof helmets covered in orange reflective tape. All had worn tall rubber boots.

"Elizabeth, did you remember the two digital cameras?" asked Angus.

"Yes, here they are, inside these two plastic covers," replied Elizabeth, laying them down beside the hurricane lamps.

Angus checked the equipment against a list he produced from his inside jacket pocket. Satisfied that they had all necessary equipment, he described his plan of action. His breath was now less labored and his thoughts now better collected after, what for him, was a long, exhausting climb.

"Regrettably, I believe Elizabeth and I cannot take the final steps over those treacherous moss-covered rocks behind the waterfall. We are of an unsteady age and just not physically able. If either of us fell or got injured in any way, we would be jeopardizing the safety and completion of what we hope is the final phase of our search. Alan, Grant, and James, you must carry on, taking with you our hopes, best wishes, and hopefully good fortune."

It took little time for Alan, Grant, and James to don their waterproof clothing, and within ten minutes, Grant, being elected leader, was soon carefully inching his way up and across the moss-covered rocks. He slowly disappeared behind the water. The white nylon rope attached to Grant's waist trailed behind him, anchored by Angus, who stood just to the side of where Grant took his first step across the rocks. When Grant tugged on the rope, giving the signal for the rest to come along, Alan and James carefully followed. Soon all three were standing close together before a narrow opening in the rock face hidden behind the waterfall.

Grant checked radio communication with Angus. This proved to be good, and Elizabeth could also clearly hear Grant's voice over the sound of falling water.

"I am lighting the lamps, one each for me and Alan. James can keep the large torch and stay some distance behind. This opening is only about two feet wide, so we must enter single-file. Here goes," came Grant's obviously excited voice over the radio.

Angus slowly paid out about twenty feet of white cord before Grant stopped. Angus and Elizabeth waited in suspense, all their endeavors culminating in these few minutes of waiting. Surely all their efforts had not been in vain.

The narrow entrance opened out three or four feet as Grant and Alan, closely followed by James, pressed forward. Soon all three men were able to stand upright. They stared into the darkness ahead. The sound of dripping water echoed from the chamber's walls, while the lights from the lamps and the penetrating flashlight beam danced and flickered on the rough, glistening granite. As their eyes acclimated to the darkness, they saw the entrance passage soon opened out again into a small round chamber. James's flashlight beam suddenly picked up a light-colored rectangular object in the center of the chamber. The men pressed forward in anticipation with newfound confidence.

Suddenly the walkie-talkie in Elizabeth's care leaped to life with a loud crackling noise. Then Alan's voice seemed to spring from the receiver in Elizabeth's trembling hand.

"Angus this is Alan, over."

"Alan, this is Angus, go ahead," Angus nervously replied, having taken the walkie-talkie from Elizabeth.

"We have found it! We have found the stone! It's here! Dirty, but it seems to be undamaged. It appears to be made of light grey marble about the size we anticipated. It's placed in the center of a small cave and lifted up a few inches on stone legs. Your dream and life's work has been accomplished! Over."

"Have you been able to take some photographs? Do not touch or move anything until you do. I just cannot believe at last our dreams seem to be fulfilled! Over," replied Angus. He looked at his Elizabeth with tears of joy now streaming down his cheeks.

"What do you mean 'our dreams *seem to be* fulfilled'? Have we not fulfilled our desires, ambition, and wishes? Is the search not over?" Alan replied, surprised. "What more can there be?"

"We must prove this stone's authenticity. No more copies, no more conjecture or supposition, and I believe I can do just that within the hour. Take as many photographs as you think necessary, but be sure to take one of each corner of the stone. We will wait here till you return."

After what seemed hours but was in reality only ten minutes, James, then Alan, and finally Grant re-emerged from behind the waterfall and re-joined Angus and Elizabeth. They congratulated each other on their success, and Angus and Elizabeth viewed the images on Alan's and Grant's digital cameras. They showed, just as Angus had imagined, a block of light-colored stone raised off the earth floor and supported by four brick-sized stones. No moss or lichen grew on the stone's surface. The floor of the cave looked level, and the only other contents appeared to be a small heap of logs in one corner. One wall had a few roughly hewn steps that led upward beside the logs, but it stopped well short of the curved ceiling.

Angus was particularly interested in the images showing the stone's corners, and after looking intensely at all four, he seemed satisfied and asked, "Did you see any inscriptions or man-made markings on the stone's surface?"

"None," answered Grant. "Nothing we could see, unless there were some on the bottom, which we were unable to view."

Angus seemed satisfied. He turned to the three men and said, "I have one last thing to accomplish, and that is to positively identify the stone we have just found as the actual Stone of Destiny. To do this, you gentlemen must help me get inside the cave so I can see and touch the stone."

"What are you going to do?" asked Elizabeth. "Can you not tell us here and have Grant or Alan return inside and do it without risking the trip yourself?"

"No," replied Angus. "You know this could be the culmination of my life's work. I need the gratification of proving the truth beyond any doubt, and only I have the knowledge to do so."

Elizabeth knew from experience that once Angus made up his mind, there was no way to make him change it, so the group set about dressing Angus in James's waterproof clothing. Soon Alan, Grant, and Angus were ready to re-enter the cave. They set off, Grant in the lead, along the same route as before.

For a man in his late seventies, Angus surprised everyone with his agility crossing the moss-covered rocks, stepping behind the waterfall, and inching himself into the crevice. He allowed Grant to lead the way into the cave, and with Alan behind him, he did not fear falling as they progressed. Soon the crevice opened into the cave, and Grant's flashlight lit up the stone.

The hurricane lamps, still standing on the earthen floor beside the stone, provided enough soft, flickering light for all to see.

"And now, gentlemen, hopefully the final proof," declared Angus. He removed a small package from his jacket pocket and placed it on the stone.

All waited expectantly as Angus unwrapped the package.

"You can clearly see, three of the stone's corners are complete, but this fourth corner has been chipped away. A small triangular piece is missing from it. None of you here were present when we discovered the casket under Robert the Bruce's coffin in Dunfermline Abbey, so none of you have seen what I have within this package."

He finished unwrapping the paper package and continued, "That casket held not only eight tokens, but also this piece of stone. You can see this piece is very similar to the color of the stone we have in front of us, and if it fits precisely into the missing corner, we can say we have positively identified the genuine stone some seven hundred years after it was lost."

Without further ado, Angus tried to fit the small piece into the missing corner. After two rotations, the small piece fit perfectly. Angus looked up, raised his arms in jubilation, and cried out, "As Archimedes once said, Eureka! Eureka! We have found the Stone of Destiny."

Chapter 16

AFFIRMATION

Time was now short, as the coronation of Charles Edward de Brus, a direct descendent of Robert the Bruce, was only a few weeks away. Within a few hours of returning home, Angus told the director of Historic Scotland about his find. Next day the director passed on the news to his senior staff and swore them all to secrecy and also informed the commanding officer of the Army Bomb Disposal Unit at army headquarters located on the northern outskirts of Edinburgh.

A few days later, an army press release appeared in the local newspaper about the finding of an unexploded bomb a mile or so above Anetty Farm. It was not uncommon for farmers to find unexploded bombs that German airplanes had jettisoned after bombing raids on the great shipbuilding yards of Clydebank in 1940. This pretence provided good cover for the bomb disposal squad to remove the stone without undue publicity and also kept the local residents well away from the area.

Removing the stone from the cave through the narrow entrance required some ingenuity. The Scone Abbey monks, without the aid of modern-day lifting and transport equipment, had managed to quickly carry the almost four-hundred-pound stone over twenty miles of rough country, but how? Angus surmised the monks had transported the stone on a wooden litter pulled by a pony, similar to the way American Indians moved belongings from campsite to campsite. He also suggested the monks then used logs as rollers on top of two long wooden rails to slide the stone through the waterfall and into the cave. This technique was often used in ancient times for moving building materials over long distances. Such methods were possibly used in the building of the Egyptian pyramids and for the transporting of large stones to Stonehenge. Even in this modern age, there did not seem to be a better or more efficient method. The army used rollers on top of trestles, similar to luggage conveyor systems at security checkpoints in airports, to transport the stone out of the cave to a level area close to the poolside. Here, once secured inside a net, the stone was lifted by a Scout helicopter and transported to army headquarters. Here the stone could be cleaned and examined more closely by geologists and archaeologists in a safe environment.

Tracy was able to return from Qatar soon enough to view the stone at army headquarters, join her friends for a private celebration at one of Edinburgh's best restaurants, and make arrangements to attend the impending coronation and subsequent celebrations. As yet, news regarding discovery of the genuine stone had not been released.

The new Scottish government, seated in the new government buildings near Holyrood Palace in Edinburgh, had long and often debated the correct procedure for the coronation of the first king of Scots since Robert the Bruce's "illegal" coronation in 1306.

Many in parliament thought the moderator of the Church of Scotland should perform the ancient ceremony, but majority opinion carried the day, and the honor of performing the ceremony fell to Lady Catherine Francis Whymes, wife of Sir Jeremy Whymes, a direct descendent of Lady Isabella MacDuff. The public also chose the site of the first coronation since 1306 to be Boot Hill, an ancient site close to Scone Abbey where most of the coronations of Scottish kings before Robert I had been carried out. These ancient coronations were viewed by attendant nobles and lords from the Mount of Belief, an earlier name for Boot Hill.

By good fortune, the morning of March 25 turned out to be glorious, and good weather was forecast to continue throughout the day. A ten-foot-high platform had been built upon Boot Hill over the original coronation site, and it was here, for a great many previous years, a replica of the stone taken south by King Edward I had been placed to satisfy tourist curiosity. This replica had been temporarily removed to make the area under the platform clear during the ceremony. A dozen steps led up to the stage, and red drapes adorned with various Scottish heraldry motifs hung behind and partway along both sides of the stage. A gold awning hung above, giving weather protection, and a mauve carpet covered the stage except the bare wooded area under the returned "coronation stone" relocated from Edinburgh Castle for the ceremony.

Invited spectators, government officials, senior members of the high court, and officers of the three armed services and police took their seats in the grandstand shortly after 10:00 a.m. Only two television cameras, one from the BBC and another from ITV, had been granted permission to transmit the coronation ceremony to a most interested general public. Only one stand-alone microphone was positioned close behind the coronation stone. An excited hush descended over the assembly as the official procession of black shiny limousines drove up the palace entrance-way and stopped within a few feet of the steps leading to the dais.

Lady Whymes and her three attendants stopped short of the steps, awaiting the signal to climb into position. Two members of the Royal Scots Guards in full Highland ceremonial dress appeared from behind the back drapes and stood on opposite sides of the stage, both holding gold-plated ceremonial trumpets at the ready. Another three like-dressed soldiers of the Argyll and Southerland Highland Regiment followed behind, each carrying one of the Honors of Scotland (the Scottish Crown Jewels): the crown, the sword, and the scepter.

"Ladies and gentlemen," announced the master of ceremonies, "the crown jewels you see before you were first used together at the coronation of the infant Mary Queen of Scots, daughter of King James V, in Stirling Castle in 1543. They were last used at this very spot on January 1, 1651 at the coronation of King Charles II.

"The Crown was made in 1540 from gold melted down from a previous crown, and more precious jewels were added. It was first used by King James V at the coronation of his second wife, Mary of Guise, mother of Mary Queen of Scots.

"Pope Julius II presented the sword to King James IV in 1507. It was made by Domenico da Suttri, an Italian craftsman.

"The scepter is the oldest of the crown jewels. It was made in 1494 and was presented to King James V by Pope Alexander.

"Please now rise for the arrival of Lady Catherine Francis Whymes, her ceremonial attendants, our king-elect, and our prime minister."

The crowd stood and watched intently. All was silent apart from the low murmur of television commentators.

Lady Whymes, wearing the ancient tartan of the Whymes family, and her two attendants, one wearing a dress of Bruce tartan and the other a dress of Stuart tartan, took their places in line a few paces behind the microphone. Lady Whymes stood a few paces behind the coronation stone

The crowd remained hushed.

A minute or so passed before the sound of horses' hoofs and trundling coach wheels approached. The Scottish state coach carrying Charles Edward de Brus and the Scottish prime minister, Ramsey Ballantine, arrived exactly on time.

A short fanfare rang out, and as the notes died away, Prime Minister Ballantine and the monarch-elect now dressed in the crimson velvet robe of state laced with gold and ermine cape climbed the steps to the dais. They stood in front of Lady Whymes. A few moments of silence passed before Prime Minister Ballantine stepped forward and addressed the still-standing crowd of some eight thousand people.

"All please be seated," began Ramsey, lowering his hand to emphasize his words. "My lords, ladies, and gentlemen, we are gathered here on the anniversary of the coronation of our much-beloved and remembered king of Scots, Robert the Bruce. Today we crown Charles Edward de Brus, a direct descendent of King Robert, as our first monarch since gaining independence. Bruce did not, during his coronation, sit upon the stone we see before us, as it had been taken to London some years before by the English King Edward I. Today Charles Edward de Brus will be crowned sitting upon the genuine Stone of Destiny, the first to do so for almost seven hundred years."

Ramsey paused to allow his statement to be fully understood, and then he continued, "This stone you see before me is a fake, and as with everything else in life bearing that description, it must be destroyed."

Ramsey then lifted a silver-plated staff that had been hidden behind the stone and rapped three times on the floor supporting the stone. After some murmurs of confusion from the gathered company, a stunned silence descended as the stone slowly sank below the dais's surface and out of view. A few seconds later, the trap door rose again, empty, to its original position directly in front of Ramsey.

Ramsey motioned to the crowd for silence and once again addressed them.

"In recent weeks, a research team led by Dr. Angus Gillespie found the original Coronation Stone only a few miles from here. That stone has been examined and positively identified as the original stone. Ladies and gentlemen, I give you the Stone of Destiny."

The red drapes opened, revealing the true stone, now cleaned and resplendent, bathed in the pale spring sunshine.

Not a word was uttered as the crowd reflected on the enormity of this unexpected turn of events.

Soon the crowd rose to their feet and burst into vibrant and enthusiastic cheering and conversation. It took some time for the crowd to settle, but when they did, Ramsey indicated that the stone should be repositioned over the trap door. The stone, mounted on small, circular rollers, was pushed into place, with its long side facing the crowd, by four members of the army Black Watch regiment.

"Now that all is ready, let us proceed with our ancient traditions. Charles Edward de Brus, please come forward and take your rightful position. Be seated upon this ancient stone and accept our allegiance to you as king and rightful ruler over us, your nation of Scots."

The End

Epilogue

Shortly after the coronation of Charles Edward de Brus, Angus and Elizabeth tied the knot in St. Giles Cathedral, not far from Angus's office in Edinburgh. It was a small affair attended mostly by close family members, but Alan, Grant, and Tracy also attended. Elizabeth joked she had become so fed up waiting for Angus to propose it was she who did the asking. Angus had smiled in embarrassment at her joke, but many thought Elizabeth's words were much closer to the truth than not. On the first anniversary of the coronation, Angus's name appeared on the King's Honors List, and shortly after was raised to knighthood and became known as Sir Angus Gillespie, Thane of Duffness. At about the same time, he was offered the position of minister for Scottish heritage. He duly accepted. Dame Elizabeth, thus titled through her marriage to Angus, became his honorary junior minister. They continued to live happily in their eighteenth-century cottage in Elgin Estates.

The following year, Tracy, Alan, and Grant also appeared in the King's Honors List as Members of the Scottish Domain. They each received this honor for their services to Scottish heritage.

Tracy returned to Scotland after being offered a position with the Scottish Civil Aviation Authority. She was based in Edinburgh at Turnhouse Airport and lived comfortably in a well-appointed flat in the Murryfield area of Edinburgh but never remarried.

Grant also returned to Scotland to take over as director of Scottish Youth Golf. He resurrected the Scottish National Golf Academy near St. Andrews and lived happily with his wife and two children near the ancient village of Ceres, a few miles from the academy.

Alan continued to live in Blair but traveled widely throughout Scotland as director of National Historic Societies. He asked that his position be made an honorary appointment and that he received only expenses as compensation for his services. He patiently awaits the return of his companion, Adith, who returned to her native land to deal with unspecified family circumstances. He only received one letter from her, posted from Beijing, stating "Be patient, my true love. I will return when my work here is done. You will be well rewarded."

Ah Ying's mother, a descendent of Emperor Zeng, traveled to Hong Kong in 1948 carrying the silver casket containing the three tokens. Ah Ying had given a native of Hong Kong, descended from Emperor Tang, one of the tokens. His brother worked in the safety equipment stores section on-board HMS *Ark Royal* and had placed Tracy's token inside her damaged aircrew watch after her accident.

Ah Ying, wearing loose-fitting clothes and with her head shaved, had arranged for the Mainland China Marine Police to drop her overboard in the vicinity of Alan's police launch in Mirs Bay. Alan's launch picked her up, and she gave the token to Alan and then dived overboard.

Ah Ying, as Grant's caddy at the golf tournament in Mission Hills, had surreptitiously placed the third token near Grant's ball, hoping he would pick it up before hitting the shot. However, that was not to be, and she retrieved the coin later in the day and left it beside a sleeping Alan the next morning. She needed to travel to Scotland to monitor the discovery of the Stone of Destiny, and she did so after becoming Alan's significant other; she had already changed her name to Adith Ng. She did return to marry and live with Alan six months after the coronation, bringing with her proof of the existence of a sister stone to the Stone of Destiny. That stone was put on display in the Emperor's Palace in Beijing.

Farmer MacFarlane donated the land surrounding the Anetty burn and waterfall to the Scottish Trust Agency. A properly prepared wooden walkway now allows visitors to climb up to the waterfall. Here a guardrail and discreetly cut steps allow safe entrance to the cave behind the waterfall where a replica stone has been placed for all to see.

.